Praise for
DRUMMERS AND DEMONS

Move over, Jessica Jones! There's a new boss bitch in town, and her name is Fia Drake.

If you want action, adventure, hot drummer dudes, and zombies that maybe aren't zombies, you are not going to want to miss this series! Pull up a seat and get ready to bag and tag escaped evil from Hell.*

* Crossbow lessons not included.

—Shannon McRoberts
USA Today Bestselling Author

Fia is a strong-willed female character who constantly breaks the boundaries of acceptability, doing as she pleases to the point of recklessness. As a reader, you want to understand what created this aloof, untouchable aspect to her. Jensen creates a vivid world, mixing good/evil, religion, and mythology to push the boundaries of what possibly exists in the dark alleys of our cities. Can't wait to enjoy the rest of this series.

—Finn O'Malley
Author, *Sessions with a Demon*

DRUMMERS AND DEMONS

DRUMMERS AND DEMONS

Fia Drake, Soul Hunter Series
Book One

D. Gabrielle Jensen

BALANCE OF SEVEN

Dallas

Drummers and Demons

Copyright © 2020 D. Gabrielle Jensen
All rights reserved. Printed in the United States.

No part of this book may be used or reproduced in any manner whatsoever without written permission except in the case of brief quotations embodied in critical articles and reviews.

This is a work of fiction. Unless otherwise indicated, all names, characters, businesses, places, events, and incidents in this book are either the product of the author's imagination or used in a fictitious manner. Any resemblance to actual persons, living or dead, or actual events is purely coincidental.

For information, contact:
Balance of Seven, www.balanceofseven.com
Publisher: dyfreeman@balanceofseven.com
Managing Editor: dtinker@balanceofseven.com

Cover Design by Adam E. Mathews, Pikuled People Art
adammathews@gmail.com

Copyediting and Formatting by D Tinker Editing
dtinker@balanceofseven.com

Publisher's Cataloging-in-Publication Data

Names: Jensen, D. Gabrielle. | Jensen, Desiree Gabrielle, 1980- .
Title: Drummers and demons / D. Gabrielle Jensen.
Description: Dallas, TX : Balance of Seven, 2020. | Series: Fia Drake, soul hunter; book 1.
Identifiers: LCCN 2020945579 | ISBN 9781947012073 (pbk.) | ISBN 9781947012080 (ebook)
Subjects: LCSH: Demonology -- Fiction. | Interpersonal relations – Fiction. | Intimacy -- Fiction. | Mythology – Fiction. | Rock musicians -- Fiction. | Solitude – Fiction. | Denver (Colo.) -- Fiction.| BISAC: FICTION / Fantasy / Action & Adventure.| FICTION / Fantasy / Dark Fantasy. | FICTION / Fantasy / Urban.
Classification: LCC PS36010.E57 D78 2020 (print) | PS3610.E57 (ebook) | DDC 813 J46--dc23
LC record available at https://lccn.loc.gov/2020945579

24 23 22 21 20   1 2 3 4 5

PROLOGUE

In a small space hidden beneath the basement of an old Victorian home, a naked woman kneels on the skin of a freshly butchered pig. Sweat-soaked blonde hair, the color of wet sand, falls heavy to the curve of her buttocks. Facing her in the dirt, a man eagerly awaits the next phase of the ritual. Light from several candles casts deep shadows over his naked form and the sharp angles of his face. Both their bodies are streaked with blood from the wounds littering their flesh.

The woman clutches a quartz blade in one hand, her arms stretched out to her sides. She can feel in her gut that the ritual she started in her teens is finally coming together. Something feels different. This time, they will succeed.

"Irzelen, infernal keeper of malevolent souls, I offer you my blood. Deliver to me warriors strong and savage, that I may remove from this earth she who stands in our way. Deliver to me warriors of rancor and ruin, that I may destroy she who destroys us."

She repeats the invocation, again and again, allowing her voice to crescendo to a feral shriek.

Around them, shadows from the candles shift and warp. They take on vaguely human forms as they change, yet they remain pitch black, only a soft sheen to be seen in the scant light. The small space grows hotter and the air buzzes with electricity as the shapes descend on the waiting mortals.

One

The summer days had started to wane, the red-orange sunset creating a silhouette of the jagged Rocky Mountains a full thirty minutes earlier than it had the night of the solstice. By the time Diane Taylor's intern, a squirrelly-looking young man with a crooked nose and pigeon toes, exited the building, long, heavy shadows stretched thick fingers across everything in view.

If Diane Taylor held true to habit, she would be out ten minutes later.

As if she had put herself on a timer, a woman in her late forties, with peroxide-blonde hair coiffed in an immovable halo, stepped out of the building right on schedule. She scanned her surroundings like a teen with a bottle of vodka in her bra, looking for anyone who might be watching.

Except she didn't look up to the roof of the garage across the street, where a bounty hunter waited to apprehend her for a crime far worse than cheating on her husband. A small woman, unassuming save for a short, messy mohawk the color of old pennies, looked out over the edge of the roof atop the low parking garage. A gauzy long-sleeved t-shirt with a hood veiled a mismatched gallery of tattoos, and a crossbow rested lazily against her shoulder. Through the lens of her scope, Fia Drake could see the flush of the woman's cheeks, which extended back to include the edges of her ears, her thin red lips curving upward in a satiated smirk.

As Fia watched, Diane Taylor lit a cigarette. *People really do that?* Fia chuckled to herself. This target had been the picture of one cliché after another. But the pause, the few seconds it took for her to pull out and light the cigarette, was all Fia needed.

She lined up her shot, aiming just above Diane Taylor's throat to account for distance, trajectory, and wind speed, and squeezed the trigger.

The bowstring made a *thwang* by her ear. In the span of another breath, Diane Taylor dropped her cigarette and clutched at her throat, the last dying reaction of her failing nervous system, before collapsing to the ground.

Fia used the space of that same breath to collapse the arms of her crossbow, jam it unceremoniously into its case, lock it up, and shove it beneath the front of her car, out of sight. She vaulted over the side of the roof, using her size and momentum to swing her body to the level below, one level above the street. Pulling her hood up over her hair, she took only a second to assure that jumping from this height was safe before leaping again. She hit the concrete below on her toes, crouching into the impact. She held the position for a second, just until she was certain she had her balance, then sprinted across the narrow drive, checking for on-coming traffic without slowing.

On the other side of the street, Fia found her bolt in a hedge, only a few feet from her felled target, a strobing purple LED giving away its position to anyone who knew to look for it. She wiped it clean and stuffed it into a satchel hanging at her hip, exchanging it for a small, lightweight collar, with tech that looked like it came from the next century.

Made of titanium, it looked delicate, especially with its hinged, collapsible design, but it was nearly indestructible. The outside was smooth, devoid of any markings that might suggest what it was or where it had come from. The first one Fia had ever seen had been snapped onto the neck of a dummy made of ballistic gel. She had carried it with her for two years. The second, she had found stuffed beneath the cushions of a decrepit couch in the hollowed-out warehouse where she used to live.

With a quick flick of her wrist, the segments of white-silver metal resumed the shape of a circle, and a copper rod, smaller than a crayon, sprang out of the groove it had fitted into. Fia slid the rod into the wound left by her bolt and snapped the collar into place. She flipped a small switch near the latch, and a green light began to blink, indicating that the tech was working and the collar had been activated.

Once the collar has been activated, you will only have a few minutes to get away from the body.

The voice in her memory belonged to an old battle axe of a nun called Agnes. Agnes had been responsible for a great deal of Fia's training and grooming, as well as the training of three other orphans like her.

Usually, Fia tried to avoid taking targets out in public. But some targets never got into situations where they couldn't be seen by the public. They didn't walk into dark alleys. They didn't park alone in parking garages. Fia had learned over the years that some targets left her no choice but to take them down in the middle of a sidewalk, in front

of anyone who might be watching from a window or doorway. Because of this, she always wore a hood to make
identification more difficult.

Beneath the hooded shirt, a blessed runic tattoo on Fia's
shoulder prevented the souls inhabiting her targets from
jumping into her body before she could get the collar in
place. Even so, Fia didn't like handling the corpses any more
than she had to, so she grabbed Diane Taylor by the feet. Fia
dragged the body to the same hedge where she had found
her bolt.

Once the body was sufficiently hidden, Fia retreated to
the garage, but as she rounded the corner toward the
pedestrian entrance, something in the corner of her vision
made the hair on her arms stand on end. On the other side
of the street, at the other end of the block, a priest stood
facing her. Even at this distance, in the weird light of dusk
and the streetlamp that had just blinked on above his head,
she was able to make out a few details. He was a slight man,
standing firmly in the range of average height, with black hair
and sharp features. Despite the suffocating heat, he was
dressed conspicuously in full ceremonial robes, as if he
wanted there to be no question of his station.

They were a fair distance from any of the Catholic
cathedrals in the area, and the outreach center wasn't nearby
either. It was too late for him to be making a business call to
any government offices, and she didn't think he was just out
for a stroll.

He acknowledged her with a dip of his chin before
turning away. She hesitated for a moment—her bow and
Scout were awaiting her return on the roof—before taking a
step to follow him. She was drawn by his reaction, concerned as much by his presence as by what he might have
seen.

She only had time for a couple of strides before he climbed into the passenger seat of a white sedan. The car pulled away from the curb, turning a wide circle in the otherwise empty street. Fia could barely identify the driver as female; large round sunglasses covered most of her face, and her hair was pulled into a high, tight ponytail. They sped away from Fia, the squeal of tires loud in the quiet, relatively empty neighborhood.

Fia watched where the car had been for a beat before turning back to the garage and taking the stairs back up to the roof. From beneath her car, she gathered up the hard-shell guitar case into which she had shoved the bow. Fitted with a foam mold, the case was inconspicuous enough for her to carry on her back when she tracked targets on foot through the city.

She laid the case in the back of the deep raspberry-red International Scout, one of the last ever made. Stripping out of her hooded t-shirt to reveal the tank top underneath, she tossed the former into the back seat. Then she changed out of her battered combat boots, exchanging them for sandals to let her hot feet breathe.

As she stepped around to the side of the vehicle, a glint of light on the hood caught her attention. She reached for the object, returning with a feather—pure white and the length of her forearm from the elbow to the tips of her fingers. Drawing it toward her, she realized the light was not reflecting off the bright white of the feather but rather originating from it.

"What the . . . ?"

She laid it on the dash and drove down to the second level, stopping toward the center, as far from overhead lights as she could get. When she held the feather down between her knees, under the steering column, her suspicion was confirmed. The feather emitted its own light, faint and hazy, like a glow-in-the-dark toy that was losing its charge.

But that wasn't all.

A soft hum—like the sound no one notices until a power outage silences it—filled the cabin of the SUV. She sat up, bringing the mysterious feather with her. She waved it slowly over the back of her hand and then touched it to the skin there before moving it to the more sensitive skin of her cheek. She laid it softly against her face and drew it away slowly until she could no longer feel the heat radiating from it, at about three inches away.

"What the hell is this thing?"

She spun it between her fingers—first one way, then the other, and back again—before laying it on the passenger seat. It was perfect, not a barb out of place. The downy fluff at the base looked like it had been painted into the world, lifted directly from the vivid imagination of an artist. There was no variation in the color; it was a brilliant white from stem to tip.

Perfect. Immaculate.

She turned on the radio, hoping heavy drums and screaming guitars would drown out the hum, of which she was now hyper aware. As she pulled the rest of the way out of the garage, she looked back toward where she had left her bounty concealed in the hedge.

The corpse was gone.

Two

Fia guided the SUV through a series of one-way streets, making her way to the busy main drag. The longest continuous street in the country, it was home to almost anything a person could want, from music venues to tattoos, hotels, clinics, and prostitutes, as well as drugs and gambling ranging from fully legal to fully illegal.

After living on the streets as a runaway for four months when she was sixteen, Fia had found herself on the wrong side of one of the area's more popular industries. A man named Ted had owned a diner with a sizable clientele. It wasn't the burgers that had brought in the majority of Ted's business, though. It was the secret menu, with choices like "Midwestern Sweet Sixteen," that really paid the bills.

"Underage prostitution," the news stations called it.

Fia preferred the term *sex trafficking*. Prostitution made it sound like the teens he hired were given a choice. She certainly hadn't been given one.

"If you're looking for work," Poe whispered, pulling Fia aside, away from the small crowd gathered at the fire they kept alive in the

rusted-out oil drum. "The diner where I work—the guy I work for— well, he said if I brought in a couple new servers, I'd get fifty bucks extra. If you stick it out for sixty days."

Poe had definitely left out a few details in her recruiting pitch. Details Fia learned after only three shifts, when Ted had called her into his office to give her her first raise—her skirt over her hips.

She hadn't been given a choice, but she had made one anyway. For someone else, it might have been enough to smash the stapler against his head and walk out. But not for Fia. Trying to pull Poe with her and seeing the near-paralyzing fear that had driven Poe to lie about what it really meant to work for Ted, Fia had taken it all a step further.

Burn scars like dragon scales, formed from boiling her flesh in oil, stretched from the fingertips to the elbow of her right arm, a permanent reminder of the day she had made the choice to put a pedophile's arm in a deep-fat fryer, along with her own, rather than participate in his "side hustle."

The diner had since been converted into a real estate office. The stigma of Ted's entrepreneurial spirit had made it too hard for people to treat it as a real choice for family dining, even after Ted's death.

Hanged himself in his jail cell with the bandages from his burn—that was the officially recorded cause of death. Fia didn't believe it, but she also didn't care. Dead was dead.

Though if her theory was correct and souls in Hell weren't staying in Hell, she'd probably run into him again.

She stopped at a light, and the feather in the seat next to her glinted in the corner of her vision. Beyond it, outside the passenger window, a side street extended back to a neighborhood she had once known well.

Seven years earlier . . .

Fia held her burned arm up to look at it. It was red and the skin had boiled, but it was healed, mostly. The bubbled scars that were forming looked like scales—dragon scales, forged in fire.

"What the hell?" she asked, without conviction.

"It's a thing I do," Poe offered dismissively, wiping healing tears from her cheeks with the ruffles of her apron. "C'mon."

"Yeah, sure. Lead the way." Stunned, Fia waved for Poe to guide her, still looking at her newly scarred arm.

They wound through alleys until they came to the back of a small concrete building. "She'll have clothes for us in here." Poe rapped three times on a green wooden door. Fia took stock of their surroundings. All the windows of the neighboring structures had steel grates covering them. Broken asphalt and gravel covered the ground several hundred feet in all directions, with only the spare weed forcing its way through a crack here and there.

The door opened, and a late-middle-aged hippie woman stepped out, embracing Poe and beckoning Fia forward. Between her patchwork broomstick skirt, flowing tunic, and head scarf, Fia determined she was wearing every color of the spectrum in at least half the patterns of the world. Stripes, checks, floral, and paisley were all represented. Her hair beneath the Moroccan-patterned scarf fell in dreadlocks to her waist. Her black feet were bare and lined with gray-white calluses.

"Beautiful Poe," she cooed. "Who is your friend?"

"Zari, this is Fia."

Fia extended her right hand, and Zari reached for it tenderly.

"*M'amie*! Your hand! Poe, did you tend to your friend?"

"I did. But not soon enough."

"Ah, well, our scars tell our stories, *n'est-ce pas*? I wager there is a good one here."

"She burned it protecting me. Zari, we need clothes."

Zari looked the girls over, head to toe. "And a place to hide, I would imagine. Those sirens are for you, *n'est-ce pas*? Come in, *mes amies*, come in." She stepped aside, ushering the teens through the door.

If anyone could help make sense of the feather, it was Zari Dacius.

"*Demons. You are hunted. But you walked away. Stole out in the dark of night. I tell you, it is not that easy,* ma chére. *They will hunt you, Fiammetta, regardless of whether you hunt them.*"

Fia hadn't used her full name since she left the convent. She hadn't even given it to Ted on her paperwork. But Zari had spoken it smoothly, easily enough to shake Fia to her core.

Fia was staring down the side street, absorbed in the idea of what she might find if she turned, when the angry report of a car horn jarred her back to the present. She glanced in the rearview mirror, giving the driver behind her a quick wave, and pulled away from the light.

Turn back, she thought as she approached the next intersection. *Zari will welcome you in, probably give you dinner.*

Not that she needed anyone to give her dinner, not anymore, but the prospect of Zari's slow-cooked green chili stew had never stopped making Fia's mouth water. The light ahead was green. She flipped on her turn signal. The next street ran one way in the wrong direction, away from the simple home turned crystal shop where Fia had spent so much of her seventeenth year. She followed that street to the left, back the way she had come from neutralizing her bounty. Two more left turns brought her back to where she could cross the avenue.

Once she did, one more left turn put her on the street that passed in front of Zari's home. Halfway to the next cross street, Fia slowed the SUV to a stop in front of the small ornate house that looked like it could have been made of gingerbread, save for the glass front door. When Zari had bought the house, she had gone through all the steps to convert it into a shop, selling crystals and tarot cards in the front and setting up a small apartment in the back.

"It is what I am expected to do, sell crystals, read fortunes," Zari had told Fia. "I do not mind. It is easy work for easy money."

But it wasn't crystals and fortunes that brought Fia back here now.

Zari had once been where Fia was, hunting and neutralizing human hosts to return condemned souls to Hell. That alone might have given her some insights into the origin of a feather that produced its own light and enough energy Fia thought it might be wired.

More beneficial than her experience as a hunter, though, was Zari's knack for knowing things. Fia had never asked, but she suspected, strongly, that Zari was psychic.

Cut the engine and go to the door.

With her eyes trained on the shop's glass door, Fia once again became aware of the faint hum of the feather.

"The shop is closed," she said aloud, rebutting her own thoughts.

Excuses. You know where the back door is. You know she'll welcome you in.

Fia glanced at the feather in the seat, watching it, willing it to move, to do anything that would prove its preternatural qualities. She sighed deeply when it refused to comply. Her foot shifted from the brake pedal to the gas, pressing down almost of its own will to ease her ahead to the next street.

Back out in the late evening traffic, Fia ran through the next steps in her routine. For seven years, she had run her jobs mostly by formula:

Obtain target.

Observe target.

Neutralize target.

Destroy the paper trail.

De-stress and regroup.

As she passed one of many concert venues on this street, though, the blinking lights of the digital marquee and the crowd of cigarette smokers gathered outside caught her eye.

Mostly *by formula,* she thought. *There are exceptions to every rule.*

"And tonight," she said aloud, guiding the SUV into downtown, "is one of those exceptions."

The "de-stress" part of the formula was almost always loud music. Her preferences leaned toward heavy drums and a competition between lead guitar and lead voice to see which could scream louder. The music almost always led to a hulking dude-bro or a dreadlocked hipster offering to buy her a drink, which she usually accepted because it was part of the game.

She pulled into a parking lot a few blocks from one of her favorite places to play this game, leaving the SUV in a far back corner, away from most of the other cars. She set out on foot, and soon she could hear the sounds she had been looking for.

As she approached the little single-level red-brick building, she could tell the show had already started. A pair of young women sat at a high-top table outside the venue, feeding one another pepperonis and strings of cheese off their pizza slices, kissing drunkenly between bites. Not far from them, a group of leather-clad teens in heavy black makeup huddled around a shared cigarette they were passing around.

Fia stepped up to the door, showed her license, and traded a ten-dollar bill for the obligatory paper bracelet that the cigarette smokers hadn't qualified for. She passed through the lobby, scanning the wall where the bands displayed their merchandise for sale. Three bands were represented, but none of them had much to offer. She continued around a dividing wall to a raised platform at the back of the concert area and climbed up to sit at an empty table.

On stage tonight was a trio of local bands, according to the marquee outside. She had only heard of one, an alt-rock vehicle with three guys—tall and thin on lead guitar and a singer with biceps as big as Fia's head, both of whom dwarfed the drummer behind them—and a girl on bass guitar. They had just started their last song when Fia came in. As she settled into her seat, they started leaving the stage one by one, leaving the drummer alone in his solo.

Long brown hair fell across the drummer's face, obscuring his features. *He's got a sexy body, though,* Fia thought. A long, noisy moment later, he rose too, flipping his visibly splintered sticks into the audience, and exited the stage, pushing between staff who had already started breaking down the equipment.

Fia abandoned her seat then and headed to the bar, taking a chance that with the small size of the crowd, her table would still be available when she returned.

"Hey, baby, can I buy you a drink?"

The voice cut through the old grunge rock now wailing through the overhead speakers as Fia stepped up to the bar. She turned to face the owner of the voice and flashed him a half smile. His black hair was pushed up and away from his face in a high pompadour, and his turquoise eyes reflected the beer sign above the bar behind her.

"Sure. Whiskey, rocks."

Her drink of choice was also a test. Straight whiskey put her in a specific category of tough, no-nonsense women, and she had learned over the years that it was a strong turnoff to the kind of man she wanted to turn off.

He stepped around her and ordered two off the middle shelf. As the bartender set the drinks in front of him, he gestured for Fia to pick hers up and held out his own for her to toast. She tapped the edge of her glass against his with a musical clink and took a long draw off it.

"I'm Carl," he offered.

She nodded. "I think I'll stick to Baby for now."

"You live around here, Baby?"

"Don't waste any time, do you, Carl?"

"Not when I see something I like."

"I see." She drained her drink and handed him the empty glass. "I appreciate the whiskey. I think I'm going to enjoy the rest of the show, though."

"Aw, come on, Baby. Wouldn't you rather get out of here? These local bands are shit."

"Then why are you here, Carl?" She gave him a beat to answer, watching his face twist in the glow of the neon lights. When he didn't say anything, she waved toward the seat she had vacated. "Good talking to you, Carl, but I'm going to get back to my spot before the next band starts." She stepped past him, carefully brushing against his arm, and moved back to her seat on the raised platform at the back of the concert area.

The biggest benefit to shows with local bands was the intervals between sets. They were small potatoes, and they knew it. They rarely kept anyone waiting longer than they needed to. They set up their gear and got started. Barely fifteen minutes had passed before the third of the three bands was assembled onstage. It was a three-piece group consisting of lumberjack-looking specimens: broad forms, flannel shirts, and heavy beards. One wore a harness around his neck to support a harmonica, and the drummer had positioned himself behind a single snare drum.

"This will either be really good or really bad," Fia muttered into the darkness.

She let them get through two songs before wondering how they had gotten the headlining spot over their predecessors, who had actually been good, and climbed down off her stool. From the platform, she had a decent view of the whole room and quickly located Carl, still standing at the bar. He appeared to be trying the same conversation with a different woman, who giggled drunkenly every time he spoke. As Fia approached, the drunk girl's seemingly sober friend gathered her up and steered her away from Carl, sending daggers at him with her eyes.

"Ouch," Fia said, stepping up behind him. "Don't think she liked you trying to take advantage of her drunk friend."

"Hey, Baby, you came back. I knew you would."

Carl turned toward the bar, raising a hand to get the bartender's attention, but Fia grabbed it and lowered it before he could order another drink. She stepped by him and started toward the door. She didn't have to look back to know he was following her.

Back outside in the close heat of the summer night, she

quickly weighed her options, ultimately electing to see if he would follow her all the way back to her car. She traversed the same four blocks back to where she had parked the Scout. She unlocked the driver's side door, which was obscured from the street by the rest of the vehicle, and reached inside, pulling a condom from the glove box.

Only then did she turn back to find Carl standing barely more than a foot away from her. She handed the square packet to him and unzipped his jeans, opening the back door of the car to further hide them from view. She kicked out of her own jeans and underwear, pulling them off over her sandals, and tossed all of it behind her into the passenger seat as she hoisted herself into the driver's seat.

"Hey, Baby, I don't think—"

"Don't think, Carl," she instructed. "No one asked you to think."

With her feet, she pushed his jeans off his hips. She wrapped her legs around his waist and urged him forward. He followed her instructions, pressing himself between her knees and pulling at her hips until he nearly dragged her off the seat.

It was over in minutes. He finished with a shout, falling forward onto her chest. She gasped at the force, bracing herself with a hand against the passenger seat to keep from falling all the way back.

Once she had regained her balance, she pushed him away and reached for her underwear, which had fallen to the floor behind her. She slipped into it and gave the back door a kick to close it. Turning in her seat, she reached for her own door, but Carl grabbed it with one of his thick, club-like hands.

"Hey, Baby, what do you say we grab some breakfast?"

She twisted her face and shook her head. "It's a little early for breakfast, Carl. I'm gonna call it a night. Thanks for a good time, though."

She pulled the door closed, waving her fingers at him through the window before making an exaggerated motion of depressing the manual lock. Then she rolled the window down far enough to address him through it.

"Might want to cover up there, Carl. Wouldn't want you getting arrested."

She started the engine and backed out of the space, leaving him exposed as a stunned look spread across his face. She kept him in the headlights for a beat, watching as he tossed the condom into a patch of weeds and pulled his jeans back up over his hips, before she left him alone in the parking lot.

Breakfast does sound good, she thought as she steered the SUV down another one-way street, heading out of the city. There was a twenty-four-hour drive-through on the way to the bunker that served breakfast all day long.

THREE

Fia crumpled the wrapper from her bacon croissant and tossed it over her shoulder into the back seat, rolling down the window to clear out the smell of smoky pork fat. The air coming in was already noticeably cooler than the heat of the city, still thick and heavy at nearly midnight. There was a difference in elevation of a couple thousand feet between the valley floor and her destination, and the SUV made the climb easily.

The first time she made the climb, she had been seventeen. Not long after the incident in the diner, she had received a cheap prepaid cell phone and map coordinates.

Seven years earlier . . .

"You have arrived at your destination," the computerized voice in Fia's earphones proudly announced.

The dirt road ended a few yards from the edge of the trees. Between the dirt and gravel and the trees—a jumble of evergreens, quaking aspens reawakening for the spring, and the state's signature blue spruce—was a rudimentary-looking campsite. There was a hole in the ground lined with rocks and covered with a cooking grate and leaves. Among the trees, the snow was still knee deep.

She cut the engine on the scooter and took off her helmet, leaning her elbows on the handlebars. "Huh. This can't be right. Can it?" She pulled the piece of paper from the pocket of her jeans and looked over it again.

Miss Drake,

As I'm certain you have realized by now, this envelope does not contain our established form of correspondence. I see that you have acquired your own means of transportation, so the next step is to get you set up with a safe space. Please travel to the enclosed coordinates. Once there, look for a flag in the ground. Approximately four feet above it will be a biometric scanner, which will read your palm print. The rest should be self-explanatory.

That was the whole note, written in the delicate scrawl common among the adults she had known at the convent. There was no hint as to what the location at the coordinates was supposed to look like. She dismounted from the little scooter, setting her helmet on the running board, and scanned the area for the flag.

At the base of one tree, a little nylon flag—the kind that grew like wildflowers out of the corners of sidewalks around the city—poked its triangular head out of a stubborn patch of snow. She crossed to the spot indicated by the flag and examined the tree.

It wasn't a real tree, but the disguise was impressive. It was only on close inspection that she realized the bark was sculpted concrete.

Starting at her own eye level, Fia looked up and down,

searching for whatever the flag was directing her to find. Finally, she noticed what looked like a knothole carved into the concrete. "Hmm." She lifted her hand, palm out, to hover over the smooth, depressed area, though skepticism kept her from bridging the final gap.

"Well?" she asked herself. "What are you waiting for? Even if someone were watching you, why would they care if you put your hand on a tree?"

In her hesitation, a memory crept to the front of her mind of Sister Agnes standing in the doorway of the sitting room, extending a tablet to Fia and her peers. Each of them in turn placed their palm against the screen, inside the outline of a hand. "You will understand when it is time," Sister Agnes had explained, the way she had explained so much of their training.

Fia laid her palm flat against the manufactured knothole, not knowing what to expect. She definitely was not expecting what happened next.

In the beam of her headlights, Fia pressed her hand against the knothole in the concrete tree for what was probably the thousandth time. With a soft groan, a section of the tree slid away, a pocket door opening to reveal a narrow stairwell untouched by both the headlights and the moonlight filtering through the canopy.

Embedded into the top of the false tree, Fia knew, was a small solar panel that provided enough power to operate the biometric scanner and mechanical door, as well as a fluorescent light below the surface and either a fan or space heater. The stairs, however, were not lit the same way. Fia fished her phone out of the pocket of the jeans in her hands and illuminated the screen to give the stairwell a quick sweep, then descended by feel.

Below ground, she faced a second pocket door, this one manual. Hauling it open, she pulled the chain dangling on the other side from the light fixture above the door. She moved a red box fan to sit at the bottom of the stairs, placing it so it would pull the stale air out of the bunker and into the stairwell, and went to work.

Inside the door to the left was a steel desk anchored to the wall, with a matching chair tucked underneath. On the opposite wall, separated from the desk and chair by only a few feet, a twin-size bed hung suspended from steel supports.

Fia threw her jeans on the bed.

A rack along the back wall provided storage for her weapons, a pair of crossbows that had been with her for years. She had gotten the first of them from her anonymous employer, along with her first bounty. Back at the convent, she had learned to shoot on a handmade wooden relic. The one she had received from the nameless priest was black anodized titanium, a maze of gears and pulleys that collapsed down to nearly flat. Shortly after, Zari had given her another, insisting she needed a backup. An even more complex model than the one the priest had given her, that one spent most of its time hanging on the rack.

At the foot of the bed, a steel cabinet held a few extra containment collars and some clothes.

In the first few months, when all she had to climb the mountain with was a motorized scooter, she hadn't made much use of this space. She had tried a few times to use it as a shelter, cooking in the firepit and sleeping indoors, but the bounties were in the city and the scooter balked at the steep climb. She could only really remember making the trip two, maybe three, more times before finding the Scout in a random driveway.

Seven years earlier . . .

She had trailed a target—target number seven, Amanda Franklin—into a residential area. She lost Amanda Franklin but found a 1978 International Scout with a handwritten "For Sale" sign in the window. She looked it up on the spot and figured out the owner was asking a fair price, if considerably less than the market value.

Deciding it was still early enough to be reasonable, Fia rang the doorbell. The woman who answered looked her up and down and started to close the door on Fia. "I'm sorry, kid. I'm not in the market for whatever you're selling."

Fia put her hand against the door. "No, ma'am. I want to buy your car. I'll give you an extra thousand," she told the woman, "if you'd be willing to help me with the legal stuff."

"Where are your parents?" the woman asked.

"I'm eighteen. Aged out of foster care." They were words Fia had heard more than once living on the streets, from the other kids.

"And where did you get that much cash?" The foster care story could usually go one of two ways: sympathy or suspicion. This time, it seemed the woman was leaning toward the latter.

"Trust, ma'am. A grandfather, my mother's father, set it up for me when I was born, to get when I turned eighteen."

There was a nugget of truth in that story, in a way. The money came from bounties and every kid who had gone through the convent was groomed to hunt the same bounties. So in a way, her financial future had been sorted when she was an infant.

With the Scout, getting to and from the bunker had become easier, but still not effortless. Fia stayed there while she was hunting; at the time, it took her about a week, sometimes a little longer, to track and neutralize a target. The pattern only allowed for a little more than two weeks—eighteen days on the outside—from the moment of possession, but she had only lost a handful to time, and none in recent memory.

Even though she hadn't used the bunker as a means to get off the streets, she had utilized it as a way to conceal her new secret life: opening her information packets there and stashing her weapons and strange abundance of cash from the prying eyes of the other teens in the warehouse and, later, of the unsavory community of her first apartment complex. And now, of the men who were luckier than Carl and were granted access to her condo. She definitely didn't need one of them finding her weapons.

In the years since she started using the bunker to compartmentalize her life, Fia had left everything pretty much alone. She had brought in a fan and heater and a new mattress for the bed, and she had hung the rack for the crossbows and a corkboard over the desk, but everything else was exactly as she had found it.

Now, she grabbed a small plastic tote containing a bottle of starter fluid and a box of matches from one of the shelves beneath the desk and started shoveling into it everything that connected her to forest commissioner Diane Taylor. The commissioner wouldn't show up to her office in the morning, which would lead the police to two assumptions. Both would be entertained until they were deemed implausible.

The first would be that whoever had abducted and tortured her interns had done the same to her. The remaining intern—whom Fia had seen earlier that night and to whom she had arbitrarily applied the name Steve—would be questioned, and the affair would come to light. At that point, both Steve and Mr. Taylor, an environmental lawyer named Donald, would become the prime suspects. Had they worked together? Or was only one to blame?

The second assumption would be that Diane Taylor was guilty and had fled the city to avoid capture. Had Steve helped? Everyone in their office knew about their affair, despite their attempts to keep it under wraps. Had she seduced him into helping her torture and murder three of his peers and friends and then left him holding the smoking gun, such as it were?

No corpse would be found to confirm the first theory. The second would be explored until Steve's level of involvement could be determined or a new suspect presented themselves.

Either way, the disappearance of Diane Taylor was simple enough to explain. However, in the event that Steve had seen Fia and pointed a finger in her direction, she would destroy any potential hint of a connection.

As she did with every bounty.

Into the plastic box, Fia swept photographs and three pages of information. She had once thought some of the photos should be sent to the police. Some she had received over the years were so damning that she questioned why the person taking them hadn't stepped in and intervened somehow to save the victims.

"Look at this one," Fia gasped, holding the photo out to Zari. They sat in the armchairs of Zari's cozy, dark living room, combing through the packet Fia had received on her third bounty. The photo she held out to Zari seemed to show her target deep in the throes of a brutal murder. "Shouldn't I give this to the cops?"

"To what end, chérie? They would first have to verify that the photograph is real. Then, if they were not already looking for this man, your target, they would have to identify him, put a name to his face. All of this could take hours or it could take days, in which case it would be too late. You would already have neutralized him, or the soul would have vacated the host. No, chérie, it is best to keep that to yourself."

In the case of Diane Taylor, the photos had included surveillance footage of her driving into the forest in the middle of the night, bearing time stamps of two and three in the morning. From those photos alone, Fia had known she didn't have long before the soul discarded the host body like the skin of a snake and moved on to its next host.

She let the photos fall unceremoniously from her fingers into the tote and reached for the dossier. Page one, which she had already swept into the box, showed who she was to track. Name, age, height, weight, occupation—what she called their vital stats. Page two was set up like a police report—and in some cases, was an actual police report—with all the grisly details of whatever crimes the soul had been using the body to commit. Diane Taylor's packet had been assembled before the bodies of her victims had been found, so her report only detailed the abduction and torture.

Fugitive abducted three young women in employ of forest commissioner Diane Taylor. Victims being held in small metal building on small parcel of private land on edge of forest reserve. Fugitive observed loading supplies into build-

ing. Supplies include restraints, caustic chemicals, and var-
ious hand tools.

It didn't happen often, not anymore, but once in a while, Fia got a bounty like Diane Taylor that made her ask questions. For some, she knew no one would have the answers. Questions like, what kind of consciousness did these otherwise incorporeal fugitives actually have? Between what she had read in the packet and what the local news had reported about the high-profile case, Fia thought what had been done to these women would have taken a lot more planning than the length of a single possession would allow.

Fia didn't think the souls cooled their heels for too long after taking a host. But even if the soul that had possessed Diane Taylor had started putting its plan into motion within minutes, it surely would have taken a day or two to transport and secure what looked, on the news, like a garden shed. The structure had been sealed well enough to be virtually airtight. Even the door had been rigged to seal when it closed. The shed had been transformed into a gas chamber, using propane gas from ten commercial-size tanks to suffocate the three women placed inside. And transporting those tanks into the woods would have taken even more time. After all, they wouldn't all have been able to fit into Diane Taylor's sedan.

Fia's working theory was that the soul had used another host until it couldn't any longer, doing most of the preparation work in a different body. The women who had been abducted, then, had likely been taken because they were convenient, working for the new host as they were. But the torture and gas chamber had already been constructed before Diane Taylor's body was taken over.

Fia didn't know, however, what that meant in relation

to her process. She had tried to reverse engineer a timeline, looking into disappearances close to the commissioner. She had done it before, too, with other more elaborate plots, but she always came up empty. From that, she could only deduce that there was no concrete way of predicting who might be next, in the event she did lose another soul to time.

She crumpled the second page of the dossier, along with the third—a list of Diane Taylor's frequently visited locations—and threw them into the box.

Once she was sure she had gathered everything that could potentially tie her to Diane Taylor, Fia edged past the fan and climbed back to the top of the stairs. The door to the outside was on a timer, closing behind her fifteen seconds after it had opened. From the inside, she only had to flip a switch to get out—handy when her hands were full.

She carried the box, which was now larger than it needed to be, out to the firepit. When she had first started, she would accumulate a lot more surveillance on her targets. In addition to whatever Father Anonymous gave her, she would fill a pocket-size notebook with notes and take dozens of photos that she would then have printed at the drugstore. By the time she would finish a job, the corkboard would be full.

Now, the box was, more than anything, a home for the matches and accelerant. Fia had a camera that she used more for the high-powered zoom lens than for taking photos because spying through a zoom lens was less suspicious than the sight of her crossbow or even binoculars. And she couldn't remember the last mini notepad she had bought.

Still in the Scout's headlights, she pulled the accelerant and matches from the box, dropping them at her feet, and upended the box over the pit. Gathering some sticks from the forested area nearby, she tossed them in on top of the paper, doused it all in starter fluid, and added a lit match to the whole works. She took a seat on a rock not far from the pit to watch orange and yellow tendrils of heat devour the paper, turning it to ash in seconds. The photos curled in on themselves, their images warping and distorting until they, too, were blackened ghosts of their former selves.

Satisfied that everything was destroyed, she pulled a shovel from the ground behind the "tree" and used it to stir the smoldering ash. Then she heaved a scoop of soil in on top of it, smothering the final glowing embers. She jammed the shovel back into the dirt where she had found it, returned the supplies to the box, and headed back below ground.

She shoved the box onto its shelf hard enough it bounced off the wall and slipped back into her jeans for the ride home.

FOUR

Three years earlier . . .

While most kids throughout the States might celebrate their twenty-first birthdays by not remembering them, Fia spent hers in the mortgage office of a bank.

She had stuck it out on the streets for just shy of a year before she started looking for an apartment. At first, she'd only wanted a place she could pay for in cash without getting too many questions but where she also didn't have to fear the possibility of contracting tetanus or syphilis just sitting in the office. She found one shortly after and lived there until she had enough money to buy something to call her own.

The condo, when she found it, was new, converted from a Victorian-era factory. Wheat flour had been the first use for the building, later dog food, and then it sat empty for half a century. Now, one-third of each of the building's three floors had been turned into a garage, while the rest of each floor had been transformed into a single condo. A hallway separated each condo's front door from the garage via a code-locked door. The elevator and stairwell also opened onto each floor's hallway.

When Fia saw the top-floor condo, she fell in love with the industrial look and feel of the exposed bricks and ductwork of the open kitchen and living room. A balcony stretched across the side of the building, with access from the living room and the bedroom. The walk-in shower and adjacent bathtub were, by themselves, as big as the bunker, another major selling point.

Though she had gone into the process with enough cash to buy the place outright, Fia elected to start with a down payment and mortgage, aiming for the less conspicuous way to play her cards. She moved in a week later—and celebrated by bringing a man home from a bar.

It was early morning when Fia made it back to the condo, during the few hours of stillness that hung over the city after the bars had closed and before garbage trucks started making their circuits. As she walked in, she dropped the keys to the Scout on the little table next to the door and started for the back of the condo.

She had picked the feather up off the floor of the SUV, where it had fallen when she tossed her clothes into the seat. She had all but forgotten about it until getting back into the quiet car from cleaning up the bunker. The hum was faint but still present and had worked its way through her ear canal directly into the meat of her brain. She had no intention of getting rid of it, but she needed to put it somewhere the noise wouldn't be in her head all the time.

As she passed through the door to the bathroom, a motion sensor triggered a series of soft amber lights lining the room a foot above the floor. They were set to shut off when she turned on the overhead light, but she left that off. Stepping up to the inset vanity, she flipped a switch to turn on the lights around the mirror instead. Then she reached down to knee level on the short wall separating the vanity from the walk-in shower and pressed her fingers against it gently. When a section of the wall popped loose, she gripped it and pulled it the rest of the way out, turning it as she did to lay flat.

She flipped open what was now the top of a little drawer, uncovering a small black handgun, no bigger than her actual hand, and laid the feather next to it. She closed the lid and returned the little safe to its space in the wall.

Reaching into the shower, she turned the faucet all the way to hot and stripped out of the clothes she had been wearing for more than twenty-four hours. Removing her black tank top further revealed her menagerie of mismatched tattoos. Her entire right arm, scars and all, remained untouched. The left, however, was decorated top to bottom, shoulder to wrist, without any kind of plan. Most of the time, she found artists around the city who offered discounts to anyone who would allow them to try new techniques they were learning.

She had watercolor-style flowers, an unwound cassette tape in the bold red and black of the trash style, and an American Southwest–style skull done entirely in small dots that could have been created using a ballpoint pen. An intricate filigree had been drawn freehand, starting at the soft flesh below her right hip, around her side, and across her back, where it met up with a runic symbol on her left shoulder.

The rune had been her first tattoo. She'd been fifteen

when a Middle Eastern spiritualist who hadn't spoken any English created it using ash and a rose thorn. She had been chasing that high ever since.

The rune was part of what she had gone through to become a bounty hunter. It had come with a blessing she hadn't understood and an explanation that she possessed the soul of a dragon. "The drake, Bel, familiar to King Nebuchadnezzar, lives through you and will guard you and keep you safe," the fakir had explained, through Sister Agnes's translation. The rune represented Bel and was intended, primarily, to protect Fia from being possessed while tending to her targets. She had burned the same pattern into the exposed beams throughout the condo and into the frame around the front door. Agnes, Zari, and Sister Cecilia, one of the other nuns who had been present for Fia's early years, had chosen to paint their own on the walls of their bedrooms.

She finished stripping and flipped off the vanity lights. With only the amber footlights illuminating the room, she stepped into the glass stall for a quick shower before disappearing into the darkness of her bedroom. With her hair still damp, she crawled into bed and slept until mid-afternoon, the blackout curtains blocking the light from the city outside.

It wasn't often that Fia had free time, though even when she did, it didn't last long. She spent the rest of the evening reveling in the slow pace of having nothing to do, no deadlines to meet, no malevolent soul to capture and send back to Hell. She even headed back to bed earlier than she normally would. By the time she woke the following morning, she was ready for another bounty.

As if her handler—her priest, Father Anonymous—had

read her mind, the familiar sound of an antique cash register chimed out across the quiet apartment while she sat at the counter eating a bowl of cereal and reading the box. She silenced the alarm—the signal that the motion sensor in her drop box had been triggered—without even looking at her phone. She pushed it aside and finished her breakfast, carrying her bowl around to the other side of the counter, rinsing it, and placing it in the dishwasher. There had been a time when she would have leaped to action at the sound of the notification. Now, she gathered herself with no more urgency than if she had suddenly remembered something she had forgotten to pick up at the grocery store.

She dressed all in black, a psychological trick she picked up from the kids in the warehouse—*"You'd think black would make you stand out, but it kind of turns you into a shadow. You don't blend in so much as just become part of the background."* She stuffed her lightweight hooded shirt into her satchel, did a quick sweep to make sure everything she wanted off was off, unplugged the toaster and coffee maker, checked that the balcony doors were locked, and headed out to the garage.

In a small strip mall in the suburbs, on the opposite side of the city from her apartment in the warehouse district, Fia eased the SUV into the fifteen-minute space outside a storage facility. The surrounding neighborhood was old. Cracks ran like lightning bolts through the blacktop, and robust sprigs of grass pushed through the separations. Signs on some of the remaining businesses were missing letters. In this strip alone, only three of the eight spaces were occupied, two of which contained the storage facility, and it had been that way for a couple of years.

Six years earlier . . .

Fia stepped off the bus, plunging her sneaker directly into a sludge of soft snow, mud, and cigarette butts. She swore and moved out of the way of the bus as she tried to shake a butt from her laces without touching it with her bare fingers.

She hadn't needed gloves today, and even just a sweatshirt was warm enough in the sun. It was a welcome reprieve after the last six months. However, it had turned the piles of snow left by the street plows into a disgusting slurry. She tried to find a drier path to the strip mall Trina had told her about, but the cuffs of her jeans were dripping with sludge by the time she finally reached her destination.

She stomped her feet outside the door in a futile attempt to avoid carrying the mess inside. Stepping up to the counter within, she announced, more confidently than she felt, "I need a box." She had her fake ID at the ready, prepared to be told she had to be twenty-one to rent.

Trina, a girl from the warehouse, had seen Fia with her money envelopes. "Girl, are you looking for trouble or just plain stupid?" she had asked before telling Fia about this place. "Don't know what you whorin', but there's a secure joint in K-Town. Good place if you sellin' nudies to old creepers or somethin'."

Fia wasn't selling nudes, but Trina had made a good point about keeping things out of sight.

Behind the counter sat a grizzled-looking woman, whom Fia estimated was anywhere from thirty to sixty-five years old. Her hair was brown and gray—not silver, not white, but dull, flat gray—and lay in limp strings against her narrow shoulders. She had a face that was deeply tanned from years of worshipping the sun.

The woman grunted in response to Fia's words, barely

looking up from the game show she was watching on a tiny television to see the seventeen-year-old girl on the other side of the counter. She blindly handed Fia a rental agreement form, shoved a pen across the counter, and resumed watching her game show.

And that was all it took. She didn't even ask for Fia's identification, fake or otherwise. She took the paperwork, filed it away under *D* for *Drake*, and lead Fia to the back hallway.

"Pick any box without a lock. You'll need yer own lock. I ain't got any for you. You got a lock?" Fia produced a padlock from inside the pouch of her sweatshirt, showing it to the woman. "Good. Pick a box and tell me the number on it. I'll add it to yer paperwork."

She turned, leaving Fia, barely more than a child, to pick out her own drop box to be used for whatever dubious purposes she might need to use it for.

Six years later, nothing had changed about the storage facility, from the woman at the front desk, to the sketchy neighborhood, to the clientele, to the twenty-four-hour access. It was a popular service among private dicks and bounty hunters, though Fia never saw any of them. She guessed they, like her, waited until no one was looking before entering the space.

Fia found her floor-level box in the back corner of the space, punched her combination into the digital keypad— that much had changed—and gave the lock a tug. The front of the drop box had a slot wide enough to slip a standard paperback novel through but too small for anyone to get a hand inside. A small motion sensor was attached just below the drop slot. Anything that passed through had to cross the sensor, which then sent a message to her phone any time it was triggered. Fia had added the motion sensor later, after she had moved into the condo, and built up some money to throw into tech like motion sensors and burner phones.

She pulled open the box and punched another code into a little keypad attached to the inside, resetting the motion sensor.

That done, she pulled a legal-size manila envelope from the box and pushed the door closed. She squeezed the weight at the bottom of the envelope, having learned over the years how thick a five-thousand-dollar bundle should be. She replaced the lock and left the building, giving the woman behind the desk another wave. As she climbed into the SUV, she dropped the envelope onto the passenger-side floor, sending it under the seat with a slight flick of her wrist. She preferred to wait to open them until she was hidden away in her bunker.

From the strip mall, the easiest route toward the mountains was an old, disused highway that ran parallel to the interstate. She would meet back up with the main road toward the north, but here she didn't have to deal with one-way streets or stoplights. On the weekends, there was potential for slow-moving traffic as people fled the city for recreational adventures, but during the week, midday, things moved fairly quickly, and she made it to the interstate in half the time it would have taken her to weave through the city.

Back at the bunker, she threw more than dropped the envelope onto the desk. "Home, sweet home," she muttered with a sigh.

The truth was, coming up here was as much a habit as anything else. *Better safe than sorry.* She popped open the envelope, breaking the seal of wax that had been pressed smooth without monogram or insignia. Just like they always were.

Seven years earlier . . .

Fia stood staring at the burlap sack that lay on the cushions of the couch she had called home for the last four months. Its contents weren't visible, but she could make out the shape and recognized the crossbow within.

She didn't know how long she'd been staring at it when a hand on her shoulder made her jump and spin around.

The abnormally tall, thin boy behind her clutched dramatically at his chest. "Christ, Fia!"

"What is it, Zeke?" she asked, unimpressed.

"Some guy left that for you—priest's collar, the whole show. I didn't know you were Catholic."

"Neither did I. What did he look like?"

Zeke shrugged. "Tall. Taller than me, lanky, all arms and legs. Mostly unexceptional."

"Aside from having at least one spider in his ancestry."

"And his nose. More of a beak than a nose."

"Okay, then. Flamingo." She had been in contact with a small handful of priests at the convent. This didn't sound like any of them. "Did he say anything?"

"Nah. Just dropped that there like he knew what he was doing. Oh, and I think . . ." He fished around under the cushions of the couch and produced an envelope. "Yeah, he tucked this in here."

She eyed the envelope, skeptical of what she would find inside. It was a plain legal-size office envelope, and it felt like a trap. Zeke pushed it toward her. "Personally, I'd want to see what was in it." Taking it from his hand, Fia flipped it so she could see the seal and found a not-so-plain glob of red wax over the edge of the flap, pressed smooth in the center.

Seven years and a few hundred envelopes later, not much had changed, save for the drop box replacing the cushions of a moth-eaten couch. Each envelope still came with ten thousand in cash—the arrangement being five thousand down and five thousand on completion, with the jobs coming so quickly now, it usually all came in one payment—and everything she would need to track the next target. Vital stats on the mortal host, hair and eye color, height, weight. Common haunts, vices, habits.

Fia usually skipped to page two, the justification, before reading any of page one. In this envelope, the victim on page two was barely identifiable as human. The parts of his face not bloated nearly to the point of popping were caved in, the bones beneath shattered. Fia examined the photos, both disturbed and impressed by the level of rage visible in this attack.

The name on the dossier was Alan Chambers. He was five foot ten, "medium build," though the photos she had been given made him look heavily muscular. Thirty-two, unmarried, with a spacious Victorian-style house south of Capitol Hill. He was a commercial real estate manager in charge of several office buildings in Lower Downtown. The historic district, like Fia's neighborhood to the north, was made up of old, disused warehouses that had been revitalized, given new lives as hotels and retail shops, with offices in the upper floors.

Judging from the snapshots included in the packet, photos taken with a high-powered zoom lens, this soul had taken its time with this host. There was a science to the possessions, milestones that were almost imperceptible to anyone who didn't know to look for them but which gave

Fia an idea of how long she might have before the soul discarded its host. The physical death when the soul claimed the host caused the host's pupils to dilate and the cornea to cloud over. A cloudy haze around the edges of this host's eyes, like the beginning stages of cataracts, suggested she only had a few days, three or four at most, before the body deteriorated enough for the host to abandon it.

Up close, the host body would start to smell like a stale attic, damp and moldy, a scent Fia equated to death. Regular people would only apply their own experiences and call it stale, damp, moldy. They might turn up their noses as the possessed person walked by but would ultimately be too polite to say anything. If they even noticed at all. It was a faint smell, one that could be masked easily enough with the right cologne or even a strong hairspray.

However, a smell wasn't something Fia could get from a photo.

She looked over the third page, which listed the places she might find her target. His office was in one of the downtown buildings he managed, and the twenty-four-hour gym he used wasn't far from it. He didn't seem to have much of a social life. Work, gym, and home had made up most of his activity, though the man he had beaten to death was found in the small parking lot behind a Capitol Hill–area bar, his blood alcohol level high enough to prove he had been inside not long before the beating.

No one inside the bar had seen anything. No signs of struggle. It was being treated as a robbery or possible gang activity, the theory being that he had been attacked on the way to his car. According to the staff that had been interviewed, the security cameras hadn't worked properly in months, so there hadn't been any help there. Even without

Fia's interference, it was likely this would end up an unsolved cold case.

Deciding the easiest place to start was near his office, Fia grabbed two bills from the stack of fifties in the envelope and stuffed them in her pocket. She picked up a book she had been reading while she waited to catch Diane Taylor, wholly expecting to need it for a ruse downtown, and tucked it into her satchel, along with one of her extra collars. With a firm tug on the light chain, she headed for the Scout and Lower Downtown.

FIVE

Fia set up camp on a concrete step with a broad, sweeping view of the street in both directions. She scanned the afternoon crowd over the top of her book, searching for her mark among the faces. The open-air mall was rife with shoppers loaded down with bags, business professionals who had ducked out of work early or taken a late lunch, and hapless tourists studying the mall map as though there would be a test later. Out of all of these, it was the suits she concerned herself with, hoping her target wouldn't be taking a casual day.

In fact, all of this was a gamble. Her mark's office was in one of these buildings, above a chain pharmacy, and he represented several properties in the area. She was taking the chance she would even find him here.

Only emergency vehicles and the free buses that ferried people from one end of the mall to the other, with stops in between, could drive through the mall. As a result, it was often sprinkled with skateboards and buskers. Half a block from where Fia had set up for the day was a living statue.

They were only allowed to stay in one place for an hour at a time, but Fia still admired the statue's tenacity. All that grease paint had to be uncomfortable in this heat. She enjoyed summer in the city—the way the scent of hot asphalt mixed with the scent of the flowers in boxes every twenty feet on the mall and with food smells from the restaurants, the way the sun made her skin tingle—but even she knew the limits of what should be endured.

The statue girl was tall and lanky, in her early twenties. Fia had never had a talent she could showcase on the street—sharpshooting with a crossbow didn't seem safe in a crowd—but she had known a few buskers in her teens. She let the statue distract her for a few minutes, waiting to see the reactions as she changed poses. The statue reached out to bump fists with a little boy, who was the only other person watching her as closely as Fia was. He squealed and tugged at the tail of his mother's shirt, pulling her attention away from the kebab cart.

Fia was just turning her attention back to scanning for her target when something else caught her eye. A man in his fifties, dressed in a suit that looked slept in, staggered along like his weekend had started hours earlier.

She watched people avoid him in a way she recognized all too well—as if they thought if they put enough effort into ignoring him, he would become invisible. But his bespoke suit and leather shoes suggested he wasn't the transient they thought he was. She didn't blame them, though; she could practically smell the cheap whiskey from across the street.

She watched the whole scene with growing intrigue as the man bumped off a mall map and into the street. Just as the light changed, he staggered into a car and kept moving, not flinching as horns were honked at him.

"Hmm, that's not your average drunk behavior," Fia mused aloud.

She tucked her book back into her satchel, keeping an eye on the man, who was now sliding along the side of a building, his shoulder pressed against the window. She found her feet and, staying on her own side of the street, set off after him. She didn't know what she was going to learn, but something about this guy piqued her curiosity.

It only took until the next block for the plot to thicken further. Another block ahead of the man, she caught sight of the priest she had seen two days before. Today, he was dressed less formally in black slacks, black shirt, and white collar, and in the daylight, Fia was better able to see the sharp features of his Aztec ancestry. Here, a couple blocks from an old Gothic cathedral, he looked a lot less out of place, but his posture remained threatening.

More threatening, however, was the man standing a step behind the priest. A full head and shoulders taller, he was almost two of the priest wide, dressed in blue jeans and a black hooded sweatshirt. Hands Fia guessed would be larger than her face were plunged deep into the sweatshirt's pouch. There was no word she could think of better than *thug* to describe the man.

She ducked into a shop, cutting straight to a window where she could watch the two men without them seeing her. The drunk continued on his collision course until he reached them, not offering to stop when he did. Father Creepy stepped aside, letting Muscle take Friday Afternoon Club by the elbow and guide him toward the side street that led to the church. FAC gnashed angrily at Muscle's shoulder, the first in this show Fia had seen him react to his surroundings. Muscle shoved him off hard enough to make FAC's head bobble back and forth.

"What the—" Before she could get the question out, Alan Chambers passed by her window. "Shit." She didn't know how much time she had with Alan Chambers, or she would have followed the other three men.

She slipped out of the shop, waiting for her target to get far enough ahead she could follow him unnoticed. Here in the crowded mall, following someone was easy. There was always someone going in the same direction.

When he turned onto a side street, though, she hesitated. There would be less than half the foot traffic there. She knew from his fact sheet that he managed a building nearby that appeared to be empty. Deciding to take the gamble, she rounded the corner. The blocks going this direction where short enough that he had nearly made it to the next corner by the time she caught sight of him again.

Fia hastened her steps, hoping she wouldn't lose him around the next corner. Even before she turned the next corner, she could see there was almost no one on the street. She scanned her surroundings quickly, searching for any sign of Alan Chambers, and rounded the corner cautiously.

The only sign of life was on the opposite side of the street, where she could see the tell-tale signs of a transient person sleeping in the small inset between two buildings. Even though she couldn't see them, their belongings had drifted out onto the sidewalk. From where she stood, she could see one shoe and the strap of a backpack.

There was a fast food sandwich shop back the way she had come. Thinking she had lost Alan Chambers, she was considering abandoning the day's quest in favor of buying a sandwich for the owner of the objects when her decision was made for her.

A hand pressed the stale smell of death into her nose and mouth while a man's strong arm wrapped around her torso from behind, pinning her arms to her sides and dragging her backward. She struggled against the attack, kicking and writhing, doing anything she could to weaken the hold he had on her.

He let the door slam behind them, turning her to face him and shoving her back against a wall by her throat. She coughed from the impact. She knew she could break his grip by shoving her arms up between his and slamming them apart from the inside. Instead, she let him hold her pinned to the wall, waiting for him to reveal his plan.

"Why are you following me?" he growled. His grip on her neck was not enough to crush, only intimidate, but she still struggled to answer him.

"There are a lot of people in this city. What makes you think I'm following you? Maybe tomorrow try the decaf cocaine. You're paranoid."

He responded as she had hoped he would. He gripped her throat tighter, the rage in the soul finding an outlet, and he slammed her against the wall. She let her shoulders take the brunt of the impact, slumping dramatically and melting to the floor when he let go of her. If he knew who—or what—she was, he didn't seem concerned. Instead, he looked like a large predator about to underestimate the potency of a poison frog. He grabbed her by her upper arms and hauled her roughly to her feet.

Where she lifted her knee and jammed it into his crotch.

In seven years, this was the first time she had come hand to hand with a target. She thought that might have been one of the supervised hunts she had missed out on. Zari had talked about taking her out and forcing her into exactly this kind of situation, but an accident on a hunt had pushed Fia to jump ship on Zari before that could happen.

The man staggered back a step. Fia's assault hadn't had

quite the desired effect, but it did give her a chance to get her legs under her before he advanced again.

Which he did almost immediately. He grabbed again for her throat; this time, she was certain he had moved well beyond the desire to scare. Smaller by nearly a foot and one hundred pounds, she was able to duck him easily, waiting until the last possible second so he would collide with the wall trying to catch her.

She moved behind him and swept a leg around low to the ground, aiming to topple him. He tripped, faltered, but then recovered. Turning around and aiming his shoulders for the center of her torso, he lunged at her. Hoping he had misjudged his own center of gravity, Fia brought her fists down between his shoulder blades like a sledgehammer, knocking him off balance. Unable to recover, he hit the tile floor on his knees, his palms making an audible slap against the surface.

Her bow was still in its guitar case in the back of the Scout, so the only weapon she had was a four-inch blade in a garter sheath accessible through a faux cargo pocket in her pant leg. In one quick, smooth motion, she removed the knife from its home and placed her boot on the spot where she had hit him, pushing him the rest of the way to the floor. She lifted her arm to plunge the blade into the back of his neck, but he moved faster, reaching out and grabbing her free foot, jerking her off it.

She hit the stone tiles hard enough to make her swallow any air that had been in her lungs, stunning her long enough for the soul to pull Alan Chambers to his feet.

"Bitch," he snarled as inhuman strength drew her up by her throat, squeezing until she saw stars at the edge of her vision.

With her heavy boots free from the floor, she took another shot at his pelvis. This time, the impact must have registered as pain for whoever, or whatever, was in charge of receiving messages, and he dropped her.

She recovered quickly, scrambling to retrieve her knife. He moved to kick her, and she swung, hamstringing him. Blood quickly soaked the leg of his gray slacks. He tried to kick her again, but the bisected muscle betrayed him, and he collapsed into a growing pool of bright red.

Fia quickly rolled him onto his stomach as his consciousness waned. Her blade made a soft, wet sound as it pressed through the muscles of his neck, scraping over his spine and skull, and a squelching sound as she pulled it back out. She grabbed her pack from the floor where it had fallen sometime during the skirmish and drew the collar from it. With a flick of her wrist, like shaking water from her hand, the technological marvel formed back into a ring. She fitted the copper rod into the wound left by the knife and snapped the collar closed, the green light flashing on to indicate the thing was active and whoever was on the other end had been notified.

"Once the collar has been activated, you will only have a few minutes to get away from the body." Agnes hovered over fourteen-year-old Fia as she fumbled with the futuristic but alarmingly simple device for the first time.

"Shouldn't I stay with it? Keep an eye on it?" Fia asked, snapping the collar closed onto a corpse made of ballistic gel.

"No. For your safety and theirs, it is imperative that you are gone when the cleaner arrives. There is never one more than ten minutes away."

Fia wiped her blade on the body's coattail and sheathed it. She dragged a large concrete planter to rest between the body of Alan Chambers and the floor-to-ceiling window and left the building. Ten minutes meant the cleaner should be there before anyone even knew Alan Chambers was missing.

Fia stopped outside the window to assure herself the corpse was, at least mostly, obscured from view. A small woman with hair the color of old pennies stared back at her. The woman in the reflection reached up with her scarred right hand and wiped a spot of blood from the lightly freckled apple of one pale cheek. The green of her irises was barely more than thin rings surrounding adrenaline-dilated pupils, reminiscent of a cornered wildcat.

With her pulse still pounding in her ears and her throat aching where it had been squeezed, Fia took a deep breath to steady herself and moved back toward the mall.

SIX

The free buses ferried everyone, from shoppers to transients, from one end of the open-air mall to the other and back again, all day, every day. As Fia stepped off the bus into the early summer heat, her heart was still pounding at the edges of her vision. She had just killed a man.

She had killed a lot of men in seven years, but she had never killed a man with nothing but her bare hands and the knife she had only ever carried for protection in case . . .

In case the target she was following figured out she was following him and dragged her into an abandoned building. The knife she carried had been at her side for specifically the reason she had used it today. In that moment, she assured herself, it had been his life or hers.

It didn't matter that, in that moment, the body had already been dead. It didn't matter because all the vital organs had still been intact and functional on an electrical level and she had put a steel blade through one of them.

His life or yours.

The voice in her head echoed the words back to her, as if repeating them would make them easier to digest.

His life or yours.

She had left the door unlocked when she left, and the tracking collar was active. The cleaners would get there before anyone even noticed Alan Chambers had never returned from his long lunch. The soul would be retrieved and returned, the body would be disposed of, and she would move on to the next target.

But she needed to get the image out of her head. More to the point, she needed to get the memory of her blade sliding into the tissue of the man's brain out of her head. The change in texture as she passed through the different tissues that protected the brain stem, the squelching sound as she pulled the knife back out—they all needed to go.

On a lamppost outside the garage where she had left the Scout, she found what she needed.

The neon-pink paper caught her eye first. Bold black letters advertised who, what, where, and when, and in the middle of all that was a picture. It was a bastardized version of a promotional photo, with all the color information removed. It had been hypercontrasted to black and featured a quartet: three unexceptional men and a woman who might have been platinum blonde in full color, with dark lips and eyes and a full gallery of rock-and-roll tattoos.

Later that night, a small venue Fia frequented would be hosting a trio of alt-rock bands. The headliner was a band she knew fairly well. One of the opening acts was a band she had barely caught before meeting Carl but had been interested in hearing more of. She couldn't recall hearing of the third band on the list.

Twenty dollars to get in, and the doors would open at

seven. She peeked at the clock on her phone. Just after one. That would give her plenty of time to clean up the bunker and wash up before diving in to get sweaty all over again.

She hiked up the stairs to the roof and pulled the Scout out of the isolated space she had chosen. She eased out of the structure and into the early-afternoon traffic, winding her way north through one-way streets, out of the city and into the mountains, to complete her routine.

Long strands of platinum-blonde hair clung to sweat and makeup across the singer's face. She had crossed the gap between the stage and barricade, standing on the diamond grate of one platform to scream into the crowd as she traded grips with fans who reached for her from several feet away.

She lifted one long leg shrouded in ripped black denim and rested a black combat boot on the top of the steel fence. A vigilant security guard offered support as she hoisted herself up to stand above the crowd, tattooed arms raised toward the rafters, exposing a pair of revolvers tattooed on the front of her hips.

She milked the crowd, beckoning their screams with the crook of her two middle fingers, before climbing back to the stage. Fia added her own voice to the chorus, though her screams sounded, to her own ear, like a pressure release, a cry of anguish more than exhilaration, and it felt like crushed glass on her injured windpipe. She bobbed her head, shaking imaginary locks of hair in time with the music.

As Fia flipped her head to the right, she had just caught a bare glimpse of the drummer from the previous act at the edge of the crowd when everyone between them surged, blocking her view. Another man—large, drunk, and dripping with sweat, his t-shirt tied around his head—lost his footing in the surge and collapsed into Fia's small frame, grabbing at her in a clumsy attempt to keep himself upright.

"Ugh," she groaned, pushing herself out from beneath his slippery torso. She considered using his t-shirt to wipe his sweat from her shoulders but ultimately decided to put some distance between them before he got any fancy ideas.

The crowd shifted again, and Fia was able to see the musician who had caught her eye before. The drummer had been dwarfed slightly behind his drum kit, but standing, he was still several inches shy of six feet. He had reclaimed the sleeveless black t-shirt he had discarded during his band's set, and his dark hair, which fell in soft waves over the floral tattoo on his shoulder, was still wet with sweat at the temples.

He leaned one elbow against the barricade, gripping the other with long fingers as he watched the headliner with a scholarly interest. He appeared to be studying them as much as enjoying the music. Fia pushed her way into the small natural voids between cuddling couples and small, tight groups, working her way across the room to stand in front of him. She stood with her back to him, dropping one arm over the barricade. She let herself fall back into the rhythm of the music, bouncing lightly on her toes, just enough that she would brush against him. She could feel his heat against her back and leaned into it. When he didn't pull away, she shifted her weight, edging even closer to him.

She could smell the wet cotton of his shirt, but also a minty musk she would guess was coming from his wet hair. Onstage, the band shifted positions, the singer perching atop a stool, the lead guitar on a second beside her, and the stage lights were reduced to a single spot on the two of them. The man behind Fia slipped a hand over her hip, pulling it into his own. He leaned down, and an errant lock of his hair fell over her chest.

She leaned back, pressing into the warmth of his chest, and let him lead the dance. When his hands slipped off her hips, moving toward her center, she guided them until she was wrapped in his arms. His breath was hot in the hollow of her collarbone, and she could feel his heart against her back, pounding but steady and slow. She turned her face to inhale more of his scent. The mint coming from his hair mixed with a heady musk and a hint of leather, most likely left behind by a jacket.

As the stripped-down ballad wound to a close, Fia turned in his grip to face him, hip to hip, chest to chest.

The drummer kept his head low and his face close enough to hers she could feel the vibrations from his voice against her cheek as he spoke. "Do you want to get out of here?"

He had taken the words right out of her mouth.

She didn't answer, only peeled out of his embrace, pulling him by the hand. He slipped free of her grip and rested his hand, hot and firm, against the small of her back. They cut through the edge of the crowd to the front of the venue; he flashed a laminated badge at the security guard, who nodded and held the door open for them.

Outside, red brick buildings stretched up toward the deepening purple of the sky. Daylight waned as the sun had disappeared behind the buildings but hadn't yet descended behind the mountains to the west of the city, resulting in the strange red light and long shadows of a hot summer sunset.

Fia pulled the handsome drummer around the corner of the venue, out of sight of the few patrons who had drifted outside for a cigarette or breath of air. She backed up to the bricks and urged him close, pressing a heavy kiss to his mouth.

He tasted like good whiskey and cheap pizza.

He rested his hands on her hips, pulling them away from the wall. She traced her fingers over chest muscles and ribs exposed by cuts in the sides of his shirt. She settled her fingers on the flesh of his back, hungrily squeezing the strong, firm muscles there.

Long before Fia was ready, he broke the kiss. He pushed himself back from her, though his hands were still firm on her hips.

"Let's walk." His brown eyes burned into hers, urging her to respond.

"Yeah, sure." She tried not to sound too disappointed.

He slipped one hand from her hip to the small of her back, gently but firmly pulling her away from the wall and pushing her ahead of him, just as he had inside.

A quiet stroll was not what Fia had had in mind, but she thought he was interested, ultimately, in the same thing she was, even if he had a different idea for how to get it done. Deciding to humor him for a few blocks, she waved a hand vaguely ahead of them. "Lead on, Macduff."

They walked in silence, reaching the end of the block before he spoke. "Did you catch our set?"

"Yeah." The word hung heavy between them until Fia realized he was waiting for her appraisal. "I did. Yeah. You guys have a cool sound. Didn't you just get signed or something?"

He blew a staccato puff of air from his nose, sounding amused. "We did. I'm still not sure I've completely processed that part, and now they're sending us out on the road."

"Wow."

"Just for three weeks. Home for a couple of shows and then another week on the road. Nothing huge, just . . . I don't know, kind of—"

"Huge?"

"I guess."

"Hey, that's great, though. Real rock-star stuff."

"Three grown men eating gas station burritos in a van, playing music for people who have never heard of them, in dive bars no one ever goes to. Super glamorous."

Fia laughed, hoping she was supposed to. He did too, though the sound was less amused and more uncomfortable, maybe even self-conscious. She considered changing the subject.

"I feel a little bad for Kim in all that glamor."

"Kim? That's your bassist?"

He nodded. "The other half of our rhythm section."

Fia steered him onto another block, now certain where they were going. From here, it was a short walk to her apartment.

Her apartment was her safe zone. She was on her own turf there; she knew where the weapons were hidden. She could see arguments both for and against taking anonymous men back to her home, and she had gotten off in more parking lots and men's room stalls than she could remember.

But she liked having the upper hand in case she needed it, so sometimes she took them home, got what she needed from them, and left them looking for a rideshare or cab back to wherever they had left their car. She had decided, in the long run, it was probably better that way anyway; it gave them time to sober up if they had been drinking.

Fia nodded toward the next intersection, urging the drummer to cross the street at the light.

"I think it's 'lay on.'" His warm baritone voice cut through the awkward silence between them.

"What's 'lay on'?"

"What you said. It's Shakespeare. But I think it's 'lay on, Macduff.' A common mistake, I believe."

She laughed genuinely, a familiar fever building in her core. "Well, what do you know? He's hot, and he's got brains in there."

"Yeah, dumb drummer knows Shakespeare."

"I didn't mean—"

It was his turn to laugh. "I'm kidding. The dumb drummer thing—it's a joke, mocking the stereotype."

"Oh."

She turned her attention to her shoes, feeling strangely out of her element. She had spent so much time with so many men who were barely interested in getting her to the finish line, never mind getting her to talk to them. Not that this one was getting her to talk much, but he was trying. Awkwardly.

With a deep breath, Fia started walking again, the fever in her midsection migrating to her cheeks. She wrapped him around another block, heading toward the final stretch.

"Hey, look, I just want to let you know, if all this 'walking on the outside of the sidewalk and taking a stroll' gentleman routine is a bit, an act, it's not really necessary. You got my attention."

He sighed, every muscle in his body tensing so much, Fia thought she could feel it. "It's not an act."

She nodded, not certain he could see it, but refusing to look at him as she did. When they reached the door of her building, she turned to face him. "Well, if the gentleman routine is for real, how do you feel about a woman who would lead you, quite purposely, to her front door when she could just as easily have taken you into the men's room? Where does that leave us?"

"I would have to kiss her hand . . ." He did. "And thank her for the lovely walk before politely excusing myself . . ." He pushed her back against the door. "For kissing her so indelicately." He pressed a ravenous kiss to her mouth, quickly followed by one to her throat.

Fia responded by pulling his hips forward until she could feel his heat burning against her. She let a hand drift over his body before breaking away and turning to punch her entry code into the keypad. He pulled back on her hips, and she swatted him away, before leading him inside to the elevator.

Seven

Once inside the elevator, Fia chewed at the drummer's lip while he unfastened her jeans. He pushed them down, just enough to expose her hips, and gripped her butt, pulling her legs apart.

With the ding of the elevator door, she pulled away from him and crossed the hall to her apartment. She kicked out of her sneakers and stripped free of her shirt, letting it fall to the dark walnut floor of the main room. She continued, unfaltering, through the space to the bathroom, with him close on her heels.

The overhead lights of the bathroom were blinding after their walk through the dimness of the streetlamps. She turned on the water in the walk-in shower and finished stripping, acutely aware that the drummer was watching her. She pushed her jeans to the floor, exposing even more of her gallery of tattoos, and stepped free of the garment one leg at a time. Then she did the same with her red cotton panties, leaving both on the floor. Finally, she reached back and unfastened her bra, letting it slip from her torso to the granite floor.

Fully naked, Fia held her ground, her back to the drummer, silently challenging him to descend on her.

She waited for a breath, then another, but he didn't break. Turning to face him, she found him still fully dressed, a stark contrast to her naked flesh. She took a step forward and adeptly dropped his jeans and shorts to his ankles.

Leaving them for him to deal with, she stepped into the shower and savored the scalding water as it colored her porcelain skin bright pink. She turned into the stream and cupped her hands beneath her breasts, forcing the water to pool between them.

The drummer stepped in behind her. He traced a long, slender finger over the filigree tattoo on her back, down her side, to the front of her hip, and back up again, so lightly that goosebumps broke out all over her body. He pressed a kiss to the back of her neck. Gripping her chin with his other hand, he pulled it up to expose her throat and worked his kisses around to the hollow between her collarbones. His hair, still dry, brushed softly against her skin, and he moved, kiss by kiss, back to where he had started. He laid both hands against her shoulders and kissed between them. Her body shook as he glided both hands down her back, over her sides, and around to her stomach, caressing every inch of her torso. He kissed along her spine until he reached the curve of her butt.

His hands moved firmly but gently over her pelvis, reaching in to squeeze the insides of her thighs and pull them up and apart. She sighed, from deep in her gut, as he explored even more of her body. His fingers were soft at the tips and calloused toward his palms, which were rough against her skin. Kisses against the backs and insides of her thighs made her shiver enough to nearly lose her balance.

A moment later, he stood and pulled her from under the water, switching places with her. He wet his long hair and slicked it back away from his face, out of his way and hers.

Fia watched hungrily as rivulets of hot water ran over his chest. She reached out her scarred hand to touch black-and-gray-shaded orchids that wound around his left shoulder, over his chiseled biceps, and down to the middle of his forearm. Their dark, delicate beauty accentuated the gentle strength she wanted to feel pressed against her.

From the tattoo, she let her hand slide over his chest to the side of his neck. She gripped his muscles and pulled him forward. He leaned into her hand, kissing her palm and then her wrist, lifting her arm to kiss the inside of her elbow. With her other hand, she traced a finger over his full dark-pink lips before pressing her own against them.

He guided her to sit on the bench that ran along the back wall of the shower and rested on his knees in front of her. She wound her fingers in his wet hair and felt his breath against her skin from hot, wet kisses as he kneaded and manipulated her thighs. She writhed and jerked against his mouth, but he refused to let up, even as she pulled at his hair. She tried to slow her breaths, taking them in deliberately and letting them out in calculated measures, but she could feel her body tensing.

No doubt he could too. As abruptly as he had started, he stopped. He pulled away from her and caressed her with his fingers, drawing abstract patterns over everything he could see.

He stood and lifted her from the bench, his brute strength shocking her for a moment. He carried her to the adjacent wall and leaned her against it beneath the shower-head, adjusting the head to spray directly on them in a hot mist. His eyes wandered over her body, pausing below her hips and again on her breasts, and she looked him over the same way.

He was thin, wiry, but hard muscles carved deep shadows in his pale flesh. A lion clawed its way up his defined chest, and the flowers from his shoulder extended down his side.

Fia beckoned with one finger, turning away as she did and leaning forward. She rested her hands against the brown-gray granite and gasped when he pushed against her and drew her hips back against him with both of his strong hands. She succumbed to his control, letting his hands roam over her skin, her muscles. In some places, his touch was barely a breath; in others, he seemed to reach in for her soul. She focused on her breathing, but the rhythm of his hips made her lose her focus more than once, and soon she let loose an animalistic howl.

Her cry was echoed back to her, a deep, resonance she could feel where his chest pressed against her back.

And then a third cry, not of pleasure but of pain, shattered the moment.

An agonized scream of injured rage tore through the apartment. Fia pushed free of her companion and out of the glass enclosure. He followed, little more than a step behind her, and she threw a towel at his chest. She nodded toward a dark hallway leading away from the bathroom.

"Go in there. Don't come out until I tell you."

She popped open the little gun safe, not bothering to turn it upright, and the feather fell to the floor. She picked it up, dropped it on the vanity counter, and grabbed the gun from its hiding place. She considered her discarded jeans but quickly decided she didn't have time to get them on over her still-wet skin.

She passed into the hallway, the small pistol aimed straight ahead and her back halfway against the wall.

Then the smell hit her. Pungent, even acrid—like a match at the moment of ignition, only a thousand times stronger. She recognized it from the collection of natural springs littered throughout the state: sulfur.

The open main room of the apartment was more shadowed than lit by the city lights shining in through the floor-to-ceiling windows, but in the center of the bare floor burned a blue-and-gold flame.

"What—"

Fia took a moment to watch the flame warp and flicker in the darkness before she laid her firearm on the bar separating the kitchen from the living room and stepped toward the kitchen, where she kept her fire extinguisher. As soon as she moved, though, the flame began to shift and take on a new shape. She watched what was unfolding before her in disbelief.

"This isn't real," she muttered quietly. "You've got to be kidding me."

In the center of the dark floor, an unusual bird beat broad wings, hovering above a flame that had no discernable fuel source. The bird bore the same shades of blue and gold as the flame it had formed from. It locked onto Fia with eyes the color of topaz for several seconds before flying out the balcony door.

The shattered balcony door.

Blue-tinged shards of glass glittered across the floor. Something had burst through it with enough force to send shrapnel ten feet into the large room.

How did I not hear that?

"Holy shit!" The drummer's rich baritone drawl cut through her thoughts. "Tell me that just happened. Was that . . . was that a phoenix? Like, a real fucking phoenix?"

Fia moved her lips to answer him but didn't know what to say. Instead, she shrugged and rubbed her hands firmly over her face, pressing the heels into her temples. What *had* just happened here?

"Aren't they supposed to be orange?" he asked softly. It sounded like a serious question, but what threw Fia more was his seemingly complete acceptance of what they had just witnessed. She turned to stare blankly at him for the space of a couple of breaths before offering him any kind of response.

"Huh?"

"Nothing, I guess. Maybe I just assumed they were orange because of the fire."

Fia began to laugh, a deep, rich belly laugh that brought tears to her eyes. He watched her for a moment, his face betraying his confusion. Then he must have been infected by the same absurdity that had caught her because he joined her.

"Oh, my . . ." she breathed after a full minute or more had passed. She wiped the tears from her cheeks and made her way to the glitter by the balcony door.

He followed her and crouched down to pick up a shard. "Bulletproof?"

"Yeah." She snorted out another laugh, this one lacking any real mirth.

"Why do you need bulletproof glass on your balcony door?"

"In case someone tries to shoot me through it, obviously," she offered matter-of-factly.

"And this happens often?"

"Never, actually. At least, not yet. I guess the irony is that bullets are probably the least of my worries."

He pulled himself to his feet, grabbing quickly at his towel before it could fall completely from his hips, and headed for the kitchen. Fia ignored him and gingerly made her way to the balcony. She looked over the edge to the street below, then back up to the sky. Wherever the bird had flown, it was long gone now.

When she turned back, the drummer was sweeping up the glass. In a towel. Like he belonged there.

Who is this guy? She had known him for all of five minutes, and here he was, accepting without question something she didn't even know if she could believe.

There had been a phoenix in her apartment. At least, she supposed it was a phoenix. There had been fire and a bird. It seemed as logical an explanation as anything else she had. Why not? She chased fugitive souls for a living. A phoenix tracked.

How had this day gone so sideways? Four hours ago, she had left this building to find loud music, sweaty bodies, and a mosh pit. All to erase the memory of killing a man with her bare hands. She hadn't even meant to bring this guy home.

He pushed the pile of broken glass toward the kitchen, looking around, lost. "Dustpan?"

"Huh?"

Fia snapped back into the moment, still rattled by everything that had happened in the past twenty minutes. And suddenly angry with a mythical bird for interrupting a great shower.

The drummer held up the broom.

"Oh." Fia moved to help him finish his project, pulling

a dustpan from beneath the sink. "You think we could recycle this? Return it for credit?"

He laughed.

"Are you in shock?" she asked, laughing a little herself. "Because that was a terrible joke."

"Maybe a little. But what else am I going to do? It's not every day I leave a show with a random girl, period, new paragraph, and then find a mythological creature in her living room. Which is gorgeous, by the way. Your living room, I mean. Not the bird. Although it was kind of pretty."

"Thanks?" She still couldn't believe how easily he was taking all this in.

"Look, I'm a nerd. I may not look like it, but I'm pretty nerdy. I read a lot, comics, fantasy. I escape into worlds where this kind of stuff is normal. I guess I prepared myself." He twisted his face, visibly considering what he had said. "Or I'm in shock."

He gripped her by the small of her back and pulled her into himself. He kissed her forehead, then her mouth, hard, passionate, hungry.

"I'll stay or go, your choice."

She held his brown eyes for several seconds before pushing free of his embrace. "It's been a weird day."

"Got it." He made his way back to the bathroom, returning moments later fully clothed. "You know where to find me."

She nodded. "Yeah."

"Lock the door." He winked and pulled the door closed behind him, leaving her alone in the apartment.

"Shit."

Fia crossed back to the balcony and lay down on the deck chair, staring past the stars, trying to see what was beyond them. Somewhere, there was a very real Heaven, with angels and deities. She hadn't thought about it much before, but if there were damned souls and demons, angels and gods went with that, right?

With her head still spinning, she closed her eyes and tried to regain some stability.

EIGHT

She woke to the heat of the morning on her bare flesh and the day's traffic below her in the street. It wasn't the first time she had slept on the balcony, naked or otherwise. Because everything in the area used to be low-reaching warehouses, her third-floor balcony was above the building next door. There was a taller building across the street, but she had put up a screen on that end to block the view.

She stretched herself off the chair and stepped over a chunk of glass that still sat in the doorframe. Once inside, she tried to retrace her steps from the night before. She hadn't checked her messages in more than twelve hours and needed to figure out where she had left her phone.

She found it, nearly dead, in the pocket of her jeans. Gathering her clothes from the bathroom floor, she carried them to her room and drew back the blackout drapes she usually left closed over the balcony door. Light flooded into the room. She found the charging cable and plugged in her phone.

There was a notification from the alarm in the drop box. She had a new job. Perfect. She didn't want to spend the rest of the day thinking about the day before.

She looked at the empty space where her balcony door had been and rolled her eyes. She needed to deal with that first. Looking up "glass repair," she dressed while she waited for someone to answer.

When she had finished setting up that appointment— two days from today; yes, they understood it was an emergency; no, there wasn't anyone who could get there faster; no, it wouldn't help if she doubled their fee—she moved to the garage. She started up the Scout, plugged her phone into the cigarette lighter, and eased the SUV out into the street below, on her way to pick up her next bounty.

Tucker Neil turned out to be an easy bounty. Clean and straightforward, the kind Fia was used to. The information packet she had received on him had been one of the sparser ones, but there had still been more than enough information to track him down.

He was a chef at a local niche restaurant. One night after his shift, he had quietly, and quickly, used one of his own knives to stab a man in the head. Two days later, the restaurant featured *tête de veau* as the house special. Another three days after that, a bounty hunter positioned on the roof of the restaurant shot a crossbow bolt through his spine.

Fia had spent the following night—last night—in her bunker, and today was shaping up to be a day off as she soaked up some human energy in a small shopping mall in the suburbs.

Fia wasn't much of a shopper, but for all her self-imposed isolation, she did enjoy people. Strange people with their own reasons for being here that didn't directly involve her. People she could just watch without having to interact with them.

Standing in line at a chain coffee bar, she was doing just that when a familiar voice cut through her concentration. "Fia Drake?"

A strange wave of guilt washed over her, even as she considered ignoring the man who had addressed her. But the manicured hand he laid on her shoulder said he wasn't going to let her. She turned to face him.

"It *is* you. I couldn't imagine there could be another redhead in this city with a tattoo like that." He pointed to his own shoulder for reference.

Fia smiled, more uncomfortable in the presence of a man than she could remember being, maybe in years. She could feel his hazel eyes passing over her, taking in the whole picture. "Yep, that's me," she confirmed, her voice sounding foreign in her own ears. "Only freshman at Piedmont High School with a tattoo."

And you, the only person there to have seen it.

Rylan Green had been the first real friend Fia had ever made. The orphans, hunters-in-training—Fia, two other girls, Meredith and Terra, and a boy, Felix—had had private tutors until they were old enough to start high school. "You will need to learn to interact with other people," Agnes had explained as she and Sister Cecilia escorted the kids through an open-air mall to buy new clothes for school.

Fia's self-assured, tough demeanor had made her an easy target for a group of bullies a year older than her, and one chance encounter with them had led to her friendship—and an eventual romance—with Rylan.

He had been one of the few regrets she had. Leaving the convent had meant leaving school and the friends she had made there as well. She had gotten her GED, only a little later than she would have otherwise, but leaving Rylan had been a hard choice.

Physically, he had changed enough that Fia needed a moment to reconcile the man before her with the boy of her memories. A heavy but neatly trimmed beard covered a collection of acne scars, and an expensive-looking suit had been tailored over broad muscles, where he had once been thin and lanky. It was the sharp contrast of his golden eyes glittering against his dark face that gave him away.

"What are you doing?" he asked after a moment. "Sorry, I mean, can I buy you a drink? Maybe catch up for a minute, if you're not in a hurry?"

"No. I mean, I'm not doing anything. Just getting my recycled air fix."

It was Fia's turn to order then, so she stepped up to the counter. "Large caramel latte and whatever he's having."

"The greens smoothie with protein, small."

"That sounds healthy." Fia laughed, the sound coming out wrong and uncomfortable. She pulled a bundle of cash from her pocket.

"I said I was buying." Rylan produced a black credit card from his wallet and handed it to the barista.

"Can I get a name for the order?" the barista asked.

"Rylan," he answered.

Fia reached between him and the register and dropped a five in the shared tip jar. "Thanks."

"Not a problem." He shrugged, returning his card to his real-leather wallet.

He's doing well too, it appears, she thought. She gestured for them to move to the other end of the counter.

"So, Fia. You look—" He looked her over, head to toe and back again. "You look good."

"Thanks. You too." She wasn't lying. He did look good, but the whole moment made her feel weird. He wanted to catch up, but there was no real way they could do that. Not honestly, anyway.

When they had known each other before, Rylan had been an escape for her. Before she started public school, life had been all about training. When she wasn't shooting at targets, she was running gymnastics and self-defense drills. It was her life, the only thing she had ever known. She had even been angry at the idea of being thrust into the regular world.

But it hadn't taken long for her to find, then actively seek, refuge in Rylan. She had quickly found that she could be just as happy being an ordinary kid, helping her ordinary boyfriend and his ordinary friends work on their ordinary cars and going to ordinary high school events. And Rylan had known that the nuns—Sister Agnes specifically—had taught her to box and shoot a crossbow, but nothing about why. She had let him assume it was their version of PE.

They took up space near the pickup counter to wait for their order. A pair of baristas fussed urgently to put out drink orders as quickly as possible.

"Green Goddess, extra protein, for Rylan," one of them called out, sliding his bright green drink to the edge.

"Soy latte for Jamie," the second called, almost over the first. A tall, thin woman squeezed between them to pick up the paper hot cup.

When the first girl finished Fia's drink, Rylan motioned toward a table for two. They took seats facing each other. "So," he started again. "Tell me what's going on. You look incredible. What are you doing?"

"Yeah, you said that."

"What happened to you, Fia? You just vanished."

Right to the point, then. The guilt returned, flipping her stomach. "Yeah, I—" She had expected the question, given how she had left, but not straight off the starting blocks.

"I guess I hoped you got adopted. I kind of always worried you went through with your plan to run away."

"Always?"

"I can't say I haven't thought about it a few times—a few dozen times."

"Well, you can stop worrying. An aunt turned up. Agnes didn't tell me about her until she showed up to take me. Didn't want to get my hopes up, you know?" Fia had worked up the lie at the time she left the convent, in case she ever needed it.

"Oh, that's good. I'm glad to hear it." He sounded relieved but sad.

"Yeah, I'm sorry I couldn't tell you. It was sudden."

"I get it. No apology necessary." The sentence hung in the air between them. "So, lighter note? What are you doing now? You live here?"

"I am. Around RiNo. You?"

"You're a long way from home. I'm in this area. Cherry Creek."

She raised an eyebrow. "That explains the suit." Cherry Creek had long been one of the more affluent parts of the city. "You aren't wearing that suit rebuilding engines. So what are you doing?"

It was partially Rylan's fault the Scout had even pinged on her radar. The only reason he had gone to school, some days, had been for auto shop. And because he and his friends had been Fia's only friends, that became her only reason too. She learned about cars right alongside them.

The summer between ninth and tenth grades, before

any of them could even drive it, Carlo's father had helped them rebuild an old muscle car.

Rylan's father, Dr. Malcom Green, had been an anthropology professor at one of the local private universities. To say he had disapproved of Rylan's hobbies would have been an understatement. Fia hadn't heard him say the words, but she thought there had been some kind of pride being insulted in the son of a doctorate holder voluntarily bruising his knuckles in the engine of a car.

"I'm still working on cars in my spare time. Rebuilding a 1940s hot rod right now. But you're right; I'm not doing that in this." He tugged at his lapels. "I'm selling luxury cars."

"Wow. How'd you con your way into that?"

"I was working in the shop. Accidentally talked some guy into a trade-in. The manager overheard and offered me a promotion."

"Congratulations? I feel like that's probably really late, but—"

"Yeah. I've been at it a couple years. But thanks. What about you?"

It was one of the questions that made her avoid small talk. It was one thing for her one-night stands to make up their own assumptions about how she made her money, but Rylan had been a friend once. There was no way, though, that she could answer him honestly.

"You'll need a story, some way to answer common personal questions," Sister Cecilia explained. Fia and the others were preparing to start public school in only three more days, each at different schools, to force them to socialize. But part of socializing for them, Cecilia was explaining, meant lying, cover stories. "This won't be as important now; you aren't likely to encounter too many other kids who want to know

what you do for a living." She giggled at her own joke. "But the best cover story is one that starts with a modicum of truth and develops organically over time. If you start working on it now, you will never have to think about it when you need it."

Fia forced a chuckle through her nose, a rehearsed part of the story. "I guess the kind of colloquial term for it is headhunter." Her breath caught as she waited for Rylan's response.

"Oh, so, like finding new recruits for corporations?"

"Like that, yes."

"Sounds exciting."

"No, it doesn't."

"No, it doesn't. You're not married?" He nodded to her left hand, which rested on the table between them.

She looked at the same hand reflexively. "Just to my work." That part, she hadn't needed to rehearse. "You are."

He held up his hand to display the dark metal band that shimmered like spilled motor oil. "Yep. Couple of years. Hey! She would love to meet you. Could you meet us tonight for dinner?"

"You and your wife?" The idea set off alarms in Fia's mind she didn't think were altogether connected to lying about her life the whole night. She thought she might have been a little excited to see Rylan and a little disappointed to see his ring.

"Yeah, it would show her you are a real person."

"What do you mean?"

"I think she thinks I made you up. The legendary Fia Drake, who cracked me in the jaw the first time we met and disappeared into thin air."

"You told your wife about me?" Though Fia had done everything in her power to avoid committed relationships, even she knew that sounded weird.

"Nah, it ain't like—I mentioned your name once or twice when we were dating."

"Name and first impression, apparently."

"We were exchanging first love stories."

"First love stories?"

"You mean you never have?"

"I didn't even—I'm still not sure I know what that means."

Rylan focused on his smoothie for a long moment, and the air between them became solid, tangible.

"Hey," Fia said, "I didn't—"

"Fia, look," he said at the same time. "I didn't—"

As they both fell silent, he motioned to her. "You first."

"Sorry. I just—wow, we were so young. But now, with my job, I don't get a lot of opportunities, you know?" She stopped, watching a wave of hurt cross his face. "You want to have dinner, we'll have dinner." She pulled out her phone to exchange contact information, exposing the hand she had been hiding under the table.

"Wow! Yeow! That's gnarly," he blurted. "Damn, I'm sorry, I—"

Fia turned the scarred limb one way, then the other, as if seeing the damage for the first time. "Yeah, deep fryer accident." Rylan cringed. Fia shrugged.

"Sorry, I didn't mean—we were exchanging numbers."

"We were."

They finished with their phones and their drinks. "It was good running into you, Fia. But I gotta get back to the lot. See you later tonight?"

She nodded. "Let me know where and when."

"Perfect." He rose to his feet and closed the gap between them. With one hand hot against her bare shoulder, he leaned in for a clumsy embrace and kissed her cheek. He drew his hand back across her shoulders and left the shop without another word.

"What the hell was that?" Fia touched her fingers to her cheek and pulled them away to look at them, not sure what she thought she would find there. "Didn't we just talk about how weird it was that he told his wife about me?" Even with the lying, she had, for a moment, thought a normal dinner with normal people might be nice.

Until now.

It was just a friendly peck. You're overreacting. Unless you wanted it to mean something?

What if she did? "That's it. Dinner's off." She got up, threw her cup in the garbage, and crossed back into the mall.

NINE

After changing her mind several more times, Fia showed up to meet Rylan and his wife, Misha, only to find Rylan waiting alone. "Hey? Where is your wife?" She set her satchel on the bench across the booth from him. She looked around, though she didn't know what she was looking for.

Behind Rylan, she could see into the balcony level where they could find old arcade games and pool tables. A pair of pinball machines and a Skee-Ball game stood sentinel at the bottom of the stairs. To her left, as she slid hesitantly into the booth, the dining area was segregated from more games; among them, a bag-toss setup was visible through the floor-to-ceiling window.

Rylan smiled warmly from deep inside his ebony beard. "I thought this place sounded casual, with the games and stuff. But it turns out Misha had plans with her sister already. Here, she left you a message." He jabbed and swiped at his phone screen, then spun it around so Fia could see.

A statuesque woman with doe eyes and smooth, tawny skin was frozen on the screen, midwave, her face twisted in a pained-looking grimace. Fia tapped the play button, and the grimace quickly morphed into a bright smile.

"Hello, Fia." Her voice through the phone was raspy, deep, but cheerful. "I apologize, but I must decline my husband's invitation to meet you for dinner. My sister had already invited me out for a girls' night. But! The man's gotta eat, so I send him with my blessing. Have a wonderful time catching up." Misha ended with a wave of her fingers, and again, Fia was staring into the weird twist of a smile frozen in progress.

She pushed the device back to Rylan. "She's trusting. You don't, by chance, have a photo of her driver's license, do you? So I know that was really your wife and not an actor you paid?"

Rylan blinked out a response not unlike Morse code and stammered.

"Easy, sport. It was a joke." She picked up her menu, hoping to change the subject. "So, we're here for dinner. What's this place got for dinner?"

They looked over their menus in relative silence, occasionally offering commentary on something they found. The conversation didn't take off again until the server returned to the kitchen with their orders. Fia took the reins in an attempt to direct their chat away from "tell me about headhunting."

"So, you and Misha? Kids? A dog?"

Rylan shook his head. "Not yet. She's in school, nursing. She's got a couple of semesters left. What about you? You're not married?"

"Still just to the job."

"I know that feeling."

"So, a car salesman and a nursing student. How did that—how did you meet?"

"She worked at the dealership when I was still in the garage. She did the appointments."

"Workplace romance, then? Sounds iffy."

"Could be. She only worked there a couple of months. It got to be too much once she started in the program."

"I can see that." Fia felt awkward as she filled space with words to avoid falling silent or losing control of the subject. "What kind of nurse does she want to be?"

"Same as ninety percent of her class. Kids or emergency."

The server returned with their meals. Fia took a long look at her four-star cheese sandwich, with its tomato slice, bacon jam, and accompanying soup, then looked across the table to see what Rylan had been given. In front of him was something that looked like a pizza assembled on top of a giant cracker and served on a wooden plank. It was decorated with a collection of grill-charred vegetables.

"The smoothie earlier, now veggies? Are you into some kind of health-nut thing?"

"Health-nut thing?"

She laughed, her anxiety increasing. "I don't know," she admitted. "I guess I just feel a little like a glutton with my three kinds of cheese and whatever bacon jam is."

He reached across the table and tore one of the triangle halves of her sandwich in two, replacing it with a wedge from his pizza. With a grin of white teeth gleaming through his beard, he took an exaggerated, animalistic bite from the pilfered sandwich.

"Hey! That's delicious." He reached back across the table, pushing the wooden plank forward with his other hand, and picked up her plate.

She brought the tines of her fork down on his hand, pressing just hard enough to make a visible impression.

"Drop that sandwich," she snarled, her own mouth curling up in a smirk. "You made your pizza; now lie in it."

He held her gaze for another beat. She applied more pressure with the fork. He returned the plate to the table and raised his hands in surrender. "I'm not looking for any trouble here."

They ate quietly, volleying questions about houses, cars, and pets, innocuous topics that didn't require much fabrication on Fia's part. When they had finished, Rylan insisted on paying the check.

"What d'ya say to a game of pool?" He nodded toward the games area.

"Sure. I'm up for that."

At the bottom of the stairs, he rested his hand on the small of her back, guiding her to ascend ahead of him. A shiver ran through her, and she tried to stretch through it before taking her first step.

She could still feel his eyes on her as she crested the top of the stairs. Moving through the dimly lit bar area toward one of the three pool tables, the one with the fewest balls still visible, she became aware of someone else watching her. It wasn't a sensation she was unaccustomed to, but this time, it pricked at her nerves.

Trying to ignore the feeling, she quickly scanned the table she'd chosen, looking for quarters on the side rail—the universal signal someone had claimed the table after the current game ended. Seeing nothing, she fished two quarters from her own pocket and placed them above the coin slot. She turned to look for Rylan and found him standing a few feet back from a pair of upright arcade games that had to be older than nearly everyone in the room.

As she took a step toward him, a hand clamped down on her arm. She looked down at it, fighting the reflex to flip the man over her back onto the floor in front of her. The hand was smooth and warmly tanned, with pristinely manicured nails and a heavy gold signet ring boasting a trio of Greek letters. Slowly and deliberately, she pried his fingers, one at a time, from her bicep, bending each one slightly back from natural as she did, challenging him to react or show any kind of pain response.

Keeping a firm grip on his pinkie finger, she turned to face him and dropped the hand when she met his cool gray eyes. She held her ground and ground her teeth, waiting for him to speak first.

He held out his other hand, palm down, fingers closed around something. When Fia didn't respond right away, he nodded toward the fist, indicating he wanted to give her something. She remained still, almost angry with him for his alpha-male impudence. He reached out and lifted her hand to meet his offering, dropping two coins into her palm and closing her fingers over them.

"The game's on me if you let me show you some techniques."

She pushed around him and returned her quarters to where he had found them. "No thanks. Maybe you didn't notice, but I'm here with someone. So I'm going to use *my* quarters to play with him."

The man with the neatly manicured hands had put an equal amount of effort into looking disheveled. His neatly pressed button-down shirt was open at the top and untucked, with the sleeves rolled to just below his elbows. Fia thought he had ironed those cuffs into place when he ironed everything else.

Or had had the cleaners do it.

His khaki slacks, also crisp and smooth, ended at his ankle bones, exposing white boat shoes with no socks. Dark roots showed in his sandy-blond hair, which had been carefully pieced and waxed into a messy spiked style.

There was a social structure among bars and restaurants around the city. This particular place was working class, despite the upscale cuisine and ten-dollar beers. This place mostly hosted state-college clientele; this guy was private university. And near as Fia could tell, he was alone. No one else was as neatly pressed as he was. Not even Rylan, who had used the time between seeing her earlier and now to exchange his expensive suit for a white t-shirt and blue jeans that looked like they had been made for him.

No, this man definitely stuck out like a sore thumb in this crowd. Which probably explained the amount of effort he had put into looking like he had put in none.

"A real man wouldn't make his girl pay, not even fifty cents for a game of pool." He reached again for her quarters.

She slammed her hand down over his, pinning it to the side rail. "I can take care of myself." She glared into his eyes, which were glazed over. *Too much alcohol,* Fia guessed as she was suddenly assaulted by the aroma of overpriced beer and cheap cologne.

He pulled his hand from underneath hers, raising both in acquiescence. "Whatever. Just thought you might appreciate some pointers while we had a little fun. You don't have to be a bitch about it."

He made a deliberate point of pushing past her, despite having plenty of room to spare, and knocking her into the table. He rounded the end of the table on his way back to the bar, passing Rylan.

"She's all yours, man. Sorry and good luck."

Rylan handed Fia a plastic cup filled with ice water and a wedge of lime. "I think Prep School there was into you. Warm for your form and all that."

"He was into being a pseudo alpha male and belittling women. Do chicks really fall for that 'let me insult you and call you weak and dumb so you'll think I'm smart and masculine' routine?" Rylan shrugged helplessly. "Whatever. Table's ready."

She pulled the balls out of their track and leaned over the table to fit them into the triangle rack. Rylan watched her set up the table, idly chalking the end of his cue. When she was finished, she gave him a moment to move, then cleared her throat loudly.

"You gonna break or what?"

He snapped to attention and lined up his shot. Fia stood where she could see the fabric of his shirt stretch over and conform to taut muscles in his arms and back as he leaned over the table.

With a clatter, Rylan sent balls zinging over the green felt of the table. One striped ball chased another into a corner pocket. "Looks like I'm stripes. So, you going home with Prep School?"

Fia furrowed her brow. "What kind of question is that?"

"I'm sure he'd welcome the company. Looked like he wanted to throw you down right here on the table." He set up another shot and shrugged. "Dominant dude, though. He might not like your style." A third striped ball hit the back of a pocket with too much force and careened back to the center of the felt. They traded places, Fia at the table and Rylan a few paces back.

"He offered to give me *pointers*."

Rylan stepped in behind her. "Of course he did. Every self-respecting douchebag knows the best way to give pointers in pool is while standing right . . ." He wrapped his arms around her, covering her hands with his own. "Here."

His body was hot against her back, but his ring was hard

and cool against her hand. She swallowed a ragged breath and pushed free of his grip. She studied the table, her heart pounding in her chest, and calculated her first two shots.

Effortlessly, she knocked one of her solid balls into a side pocket, and the cue ball rolled to a stop only an inch from another solid, right where she had planned. She repositioned and struck the egg-colored globe, putting not one but two of her balls into two different holes. Moving again to the other side of the table, she reached out with her cue and tapped it against the corner pocket. With a sharp *clack*, a fourth ball vanished into the abyss.

"Hey, it's cool. You play, I'll watch. I'm good over here," Rylan snarked, setting another pair of quarters on the table before climbing onto a nearby bistro chair. The next sentence came out in a low growl, barely above a sigh. "I'm so good just watching from here."

Her last three balls were gone in two more turns, and she tapped her cue against the table again, this time on the side pocket. "Eight ball, side pocket."

"Sure. They were your quarters anyway."

Before she leaned into her shot, Fia stole a quick look in his direction, watching as he wrung his hands over the length of his cue stick. Fever passed through her, and she closed her eyes, trying to redirect her focus to the black ball taunting her from a few feet away. She opened her eyes and dipped her shoulder into her stick. There was a *swish* as the cue ball moved over the felt and a *clack* as it connected with the eight ball, stopping short and sending the black ball forward into the side pocket, where Rylan's quarters sat on the rail.

Rylan lowered himself from the high chair and crossed the space to the table, reaching for the coins to put them in the slot.

Fia got to them first, picking them up and dropping them in his front pocket. "I don't think another game is a good idea. Go home. Give your wife some of that heat."

Injured rejection washed over his face, followed by the realization that she was right. He pulled her into a hug. "Thanks, Fia. Maybe we can get together again."

Probably not. "Yeah, maybe."

"You're good to get home?"

"Golden. Go."

She watched as he headed for the stairs. He stopped to let a woman go ahead of him, her long dark-blonde ponytail swaying slightly as she disappeared from view. As Rylan started down the stairs, Fia glanced around and spotted Prep School near the bar. Making a decision, she squatted down beside the table to untie and loosen her boots. Then she made her way to the bar, putting four barstools between them, and ordered herself a shot of whiskey.

"You should have let him win." Fia was impressed to hear Prep School was just sober enough that most of his words were still independent of the others.

"What?"

"Guys don't like to be beaten by chicks. I'm Brent, by the way."

Of course he was. She thought the only way he could have been more cliché was if he had told her his name was Kip. Brent Kipman, she decided, staring at him and studying his entitled face for a long second before letting her eyes trace his torso down to his perfectly pressed khakis. She threw back her shot and took one of his well-manicured hands, pulling him away from the bar. Maybe Rylan was right; maybe the answer to this guy's problem was in being dominated. Hard.

She led him away from the bar and back downstairs to

the men's room. There was no door, just a labyrinthine hallway opening into a large empty space that was lined on one side with urinals and black matte stalls on the other.

She pulled him to the stall farthest from the entrance and locked them both inside, resting her shoulder bag on the back of the toilet. He leaned in for a beer-soaked kiss, but she pushed him away, snapping a condom from inside the bag into his hand. She deftly unfastened his khakis, letting them fall to the filthy floor, and then kicked out of her boots, stuffed her socks inside them, and laid her jeans and underwear on top of her bag.

He picked her up, pressing her into the wall and wedging himself between her and the toilet. She braced herself with her feet on the seat while he humped at her drunkenly. He hadn't seemed quite this inebriated in the dim light of the bar. He had certainly put on a good show because now he was all but drooling on her. He smelled even worse than he had before; a bouquet of hot craft beer seemed to be coming from his pores, and it smelled like he had applied more of his cheap cologne. And now sweat. The back of his perfectly arranged shirt was already soaked through.

Certain he was going to finish before she even got started, she tried to push him away.

Instead of backing away, he moved his hands from her hips to her throat, squeezing so hard it hurt when she tried to breathe. He continued thrusting hard against her, his eyes flashing wildly. Each thrust was harder than the one before, and he grunted with each. She coughed uselessly, clawing at anything she could reach. She dug her thumbs into his eyes, and he howled in pain but refused to let go of her throat.

As her lungs joined the protest, Fia's vision started to darken, but something caught the edge of her sight. Coat hook. The brushed-silver hardware dangled from one precarious screw, barely within her reach. She swung her arm once for it, missing, and tried again. With the last ounce of strength she could find, she ripped it from the steel door and buried it in the side of Brent's neck in one swift motion.

That was what it took to get him to finally release his grip on her neck. He staggered backward, fell over the porcelain, and slammed his back and head against the bricks with a crack, leaving a red smear as he slid down.

His tidy hands pawed frantically at the foreign object in his neck. When he finally found it and removed it, he and Fia both discovered it had been the last thing keeping his blood in his body. Dark red fluid soaked the front of his shirt, and his limbs went slack, his eyes rolling up to look at the ceiling. He folded, slipping the rest of the way between the toilet and the wall, his feet on the seat and his perfectly pressed pants where she had left them around his ankles.

As he lost consciousness, Fia stuffed her pants and boots into her canvas bag, slinging it across her torso. As a last-second thought, she removed the condom, wrapped it in toilet paper, and put it and the silver hook in the little side pocket of her satchel. Then she jumped, hooking her fingers over the ledge of the small window set high in the wall, climbed her feet up the wall, and slipped through the small space, dropping to the pavement below.

Ten

Outside, the air was hot and stagnant, like an oven, and the asphalt stung the bottom of her bare feet. Fia shimmied back into her jeans, knocking a piece of broken glass off the heel of her right foot, and put her boots back on, though she left them untied. She stuffed her socks into her jeans pocket.

As she straightened, the light of a streetlamp caught on a red-black stain on her shirt. She stripped free of it and used it to wipe her face, which was soaked with sweat and spattered with someone else's blood for the second time in a week.

Out in the parking lot next to the bar, she flipped up the seat of her glittery red Vespa Sprint and stuffed the bloodstained garment inside. She exchanged it for a black t-shirt that was wrinkled from being in the compartment for who knew how long. She had cut the collar and sleeves off ages ago, leaving behind the worn white image of a girl with a mohawk. The cotton smelled stale, but it was clean.

Fia secured her helmet over her short red hair and eased the scooter into traffic. As she did, she narrowly missed colliding with the woman with the high ponytail who was walking into the lot, her phone pressed to her ear and partially obscuring her face. Deeply engrossed in her phone call, the woman didn't even seem to notice Fia.

Fia's nerves were shot. The last place she thought she should be was alone in her apartment. She considered, for a moment, the prospect of spending the night in her bunker but decided that wouldn't be any better. She would still be alone with the night.

Alan Chambers had tried to kill her. He had held her off the ground by her throat, determined to end her life by crushing her windpipe. Her throat had ached for hours after, and she was more than a little surprised he hadn't left a hand-shaped bruise. For the first time ever, she had put her knife in the back of a human skull.

But that had been work. She had left the bunker that day knowing she was in pursuit of a bounty. The corpse she had left had been a corpse she had intended to leave. It was only the up-close nature of the kill, the memory of steel scraping on bone, and her own brush with death that had bothered her.

This guy, this trust-fund kid, had tried to kill her and in almost the same way. Hands around her throat, squeezing off her oxygen. It had been no less a question of his life or hers, but somehow, knowing she had chosen to lead him into that stall—into her—almost made putting that hook through his neck as much a choice as anything she had done up to that point.

Could she have gotten away without such a drastic response? She had clawed at his eyes without fazing him. *He was going to kill you. In cold blood. And get off when he did. There was no stopping him.*

Fia aimlessly followed one-way streets back and forth

until she found herself idling the scooter in the street outside the bar she had visited after neutralizing Diane Taylor's possession. She pulled the hook out of the little pocket she'd shoved it in, dropping her satchel into the cargo of the scooter. By now, she had handled the hook enough that it had been wiped clean of most of the blood. She gave it one more quick wipe on her jeans. Even if someone found it here, she had traveled far enough from the body of Brent Kipman that no one would likely make the connection, but removing her fingerprints made her feel better anyway.

She would get rid of his DNA somewhere else. Just in case.

She dropped the hook into a garbage can just outside the bar and stepped up to the short queue waiting to go inside. The man positioned outside the door wore a sober expression on his dark face, all business as he checked IDs and strapped on paper bracelets. He recognized Fia as a regular and waved away her outstretched driver's license, dropping her cover charge into the bucket and handing her a bracelet.

Inside, the music was too loud to expect conversation from anyone, and that was just fine with Fia. She took a seat at the end of the bar closest to the door and ordered her go-to for drinking alone, whiskey and cola. Her first swallow delivered an anesthetic burn to her injured throat.

The music blaring through the overhead speakers softened. The house lights dimmed, calling attention to the stage lights. Fia obliged and turned on her stool to face the light. A sound effects MIDI track warbled through the speakers as CO_2 fog spread across the stage. As the first musician stepped onto the stage to take his place on his throne, Fia heard a strange sound emerge from her throat: a blend of panic, surprise, and delight.

His lithe frame was partially obscured by a cymbal and tom, but her view was perfect for her to watch him tuck his golden-brown waves loosely behind his ears, adjust his earpieces, and make quick hand gestures to the sound guy.

It's a coincidence, a rational voice spoke up inside her head. *He's in a local band that plays in the places where you like to see bands and pick up men. You've probably seen him before; he just got in your head, and now you're hyperaware of him.*

She only realized her heart had been pounding in her ears when it was replaced with the steady *thump-thump* of his bass drum. She finally released the last breath she had taken in before Prep School Brent almost came trying to steal it away from her. Her taut muscles began to relax, and she could feel where her nails had been digging into the palm of her left hand. She turned it over to see three angry crescents glaring back at her and tried to rub them out with the other hand, finally pressing her palm into the side of her cold glass.

She let her eyes track back to the stage.

His arms were raised above his head, clapping his hands for the crowd to join him. She did, slapping her free hand against her thigh, and let her chin fall to her chest, her eyes closed. The music washed over her.

When they finished, Fia turned to the bartender. "How often do they play here?"

"Couple times a month. Big dude's friends with one of the managers. I guess they just got some kind of contract a while back." She pointed at Fia's empty glass. "Jack and Coke?"

Fia wasn't staying. She didn't think she could after all that had gone down tonight. Seeing the drummer on the stage made her feel guilty about Brent in a whole different way, and she didn't like that. Or need it. She didn't mind watching his form for a little while, but she needed to hit the pavement before he saw her. Back here in the corner, she was obscured by shadows, and he had lights in his face.

She nodded to the bartender, a young girl, probably a college student, with a black-dyed 40s pinup bob and ruby lips to match. "Hold the Jack."

"Got it, gorgeous." The bartender poured the cola and slid it to her with a wink. She saw where Fia's eyes were trained and leaned in closer. "Drummer's cute, yeah? Seems like kind of a jerk, though. Really aloof. Single, I think. Only one who never has a girl at these shows. No charge for the coke."

Fia pushed a five across the bar to her and waved for her to keep it. Aloof, huh? Yeah, maybe. It must be an act, though. A stage persona. She hadn't gotten that impression at all. He had seemed pretty chill, even nice.

She jabbed at an ice cube with the straw and took a long pull, draining a third of the liquid from the glass. What was she doing? She needed to get out of here.

She finished her drink and the song and got up to leave. The familiar bell of an antique cash register rang from her pocket, and she breathed a sigh of relief. She didn't think she had ever wanted a job more than she did in this moment.

ELEVEN

Fia had decided years ago that she didn't need to watch the news or read the papers. She knew a lot of the worst stories even before the police did and especially before the news directors. And the stories she didn't know, she didn't want to know.

But this time, she wasn't waiting around to find out what she already knew. She waited in the city until she could catch the morning news and find out what had happened after she left. After getting the alert that she had a new bounty, she had gone back to her apartment to trade the scooter for her SUV, before going to the storage unit and then sleeping a few hours in the back seat while she waited for the news.

She had found a small café where she could do that. She tried to put away a couple strips of bacon and some coffee while she watched the pretty anchorwoman feign shock and horror as she read from the teleprompter.

"Brent Newman, CEO of Newman Robotics, was found dead last night at a local restaurant after an anonymous call to 911. Newman was stabbed, in what police are calling a crime of opportunity. No weapon was found at or near the scene, and according to police, his wallet and any jewelry he might have been wearing had been removed. Police are investigating the case as a robbery-turned-homicide. Investigators are asking anyone with information regarding this crime to please contact the department directly."

Well, they're half right, Fia thought, nibbling on the bacon but not tasting it. It had been a crime of opportunity. She remembered the woman in the parking lot who'd been talking on her phone when Fia nearly hit her. Had she been on the phone with dispatchers at that exact moment? She had been so deeply engrossed in her call that she hadn't even acknowledged Fia, but she had been calm. She hadn't shown any outward signs that she had just found a blood-soaked corpse in a public restroom.

A public men's restroom.

There were bits of the news report that didn't line up, of course. As far as Fia knew, the man she had left dead on the restroom floor had still had his wallet—unless he had never had one—and she had definitely left behind that gawdy signet ring. The best explanation she had was that the woman who had made the 911 call had taken those things.

But why?

She pushed the question from her mind; more likely than not, she would never know the answer. For now, she decided to feel relief that someone had taken those things, for whatever reason, and now the police were on a goose chase.

The television screen flashed from the anchorwoman to a scene of kids flying kites in a neighborhood park, and Fia drained her coffee. She ran through her usual routine, calculating the total for the bill she hadn't yet received, rounding each item up to account for tax, and throwing in a few extra dollars for tip. She left ten on the table and slipped out of the café.

She climbed into the Scout, reaching beneath her seat to make sure the envelope was still there, and coaxed the vehicle to life.

The trip to the bunker was made by muscle memory, and soon she was buried deep underground, away from whoever might have seen her go into that restroom with Brent Newman last night and called the police.

She pulled the dossier from the envelope and swore.

Staring back at her from a publicity headshot were the gray eyes of Brent Newman, CEO of Newman Robotics, recently dead from a crime of opportunity.

The relief Fia had felt after the earlier news report evaporated.

She had gotten her bounty, all right. She had stabbed him in the carotid artery with a coat hook and every ounce of strength she had before he could choke her unconscious. But she hadn't known he had been possessed and therefore hadn't even thought of containing the soul that likely now inhabited someone who had been in that restaurant last night. Maybe even the woman who had called in the crime. Which was little comfort when Fia would never be able to find out who that was.

This particular soul almost murdered you.

Fia didn't like that either.

She didn't know what she was supposed to do now. The hands-off, no-contact method she had used to communicate with Father (or Fathers) Anonymous over the years had left her mostly on her own.

If nothing else, activate the collar, leave it out of sight, and run.

That advice had worked for Zari on at least one occasion. It was even how Fia had passed on the news about her drop box. She had burned a collar, activating it and leaving it under a dumpster that had been repurposed for free clothing, along with the address of the rental space and a request for another collar.

Now the collars were on a replenishment subscription. She would use three or four and three or four more would show up in the box. She had been wary of sharing the lock's combination with a stranger, but she couldn't continue to let Father Anonymous wander into camp every week. Even if a priest would have been one of the least conspicuous outsiders there.

Fia pushed the money and the dossier to the back of the desk—an act of avoidance more than anything—and retreated to the twin-size bunk. What had started out as a fun night reconnecting with an old friend had gone really wrong, really fast. But it felt like everything lately was going that way.

Alan Chambers.

That drummer in her head.

That fucking bird.

And now Brent Newman, dead of apparent robbery in a bar he hadn't even belonged in.

She decided to sleep now and figure out what to do about him later.

Except she couldn't sleep. For twenty minutes, she lay in the bunk with her eyes closed, focusing on her breathing, her throat still screaming where he had tried to crush it. Finally, she got back up and retrieved the dossier, flipping to the second page, the way she always did with a new bounty. She wanted to know what they had done to justify putting a bolt in their spine.

The soul in charge of Brent Newman's body had apparently been a sexually motivated rage killer in his original existence, if the idea that the evil traveled with the soul was accurate. Three girls had been found in the same condition Fia had narrowly avoided. The sex had appeared consensual, but the examiner's report suggested that erotic asphyxiation had turned bad, that the murders had happened midcoitus. Fia gently touched her tender hyoid and remembered the look of horror on Brent's face as he grabbed uselessly at the hook in his neck.

Self-defense.

Except she had lured him into the restroom. She had encouraged sex. It was her word against his . . .

She hoped against everything that the police continued to treat it as a robbery gone sideways. She ran through the injuries she had inflicted. His eyes would be bruised where she had pressed her thumbs into them—*Do eyeballs bruise?*—and his head had split open when he hit it against the bricks.

"You should see the other guy," she muttered to the empty room.

She gathered up the cash and the dossier, pulled a containment collar from her cabinet, and headed back into the city. In the alley where she had landed after climbing out the window, she laid the envelope with the cash and dossier on the ground beneath a dumpster and surrounded them with the collar, the green tracking light sparking to life as the lock engaged.

Ten minutes.

She reached back into the envelope, pulled out the dossier, and scribbled on the front page: *DOA. Target not obtained.* She put everything back and walked away, her heart pounding hard enough to make her feel sick.

Twelve

Fia leaned on the short wall surrounding the top level of a parking garage, her arms dangling over the sides. The afternoon sun cooked into the black cotton hood concealing her hair. Her scalp itched from the heat.

A containment collar lay on the ledge to her left, while her bow stood against the wall to her right. Across the street, five stories below, a small group of city maintenance workers milled around, milking the time clock until their five o'clock quitting time. Her target, a forty-year-old man named Tyler Jacobson, was among them.

Tyler Jacobson was more the kind of target Fia was accustomed to. He'd worked a dozen different jobs in manual labor over the past decade, losing them for performance reasons that ranged from not showing up to one incident of putting a supervisor in the hospital after a disagreement. In fact, given his volatile record, Fia had questioned whether the possession was legitimate.

Sometimes, adding a before picture to the packet wasn't possible; other times, it seemed that Father Anonymous couldn't get close enough for the after picture. This had been one of the latter cases, so Fia had stepped in front of Tyler Jacobson as he came out of an alley where he'd been working, forcing a collision so she could look into his eyes. She had taken the chance that being on the street during business hours would keep his temper in check.

Now certain she had a legitimate possession in her crosshairs, Fia watched from above as two of the four men loaded their tools into one of the waiting vehicles. They climbed in and drove away, leaving Tyler Jacobson and the fourth man to clean up the remainder of the jobsite. The fourth man was young; this was probably his first job.

Fia kept her eyes on her target. Her plan was to follow him when he left the job. She had left the door to the Scout open, just in case she had to make a quick break, though she didn't really expect that. More likely, Tyler Jacobson and his young partner would simply load up, just as the other two had done, and drive calmly away.

She stood upright and reached for her weapon.

So did Tyler Jacobson.

Fia felt the hair prickle at the back of her neck as he stepped up to the truck behind the kid, pulling out a hammer the kid had just put away.

She jerked the crossbow up to rest it on the wall where she had been leaning.

Tyler Jacobson drew back his right arm.

She worked to find a clear line of fire where she wouldn't hit the kid.

The *thwang* of the bowstring rang in Fia's ear, and she thought she heard the crack of the hammer against the kid's skull.

Both men crumbled to the asphalt, and Fia began her descent.

After leaving the convent, and subsequently the gymnastics training she had been getting there, she took to teaching herself parkour. The two skills combined allowed her to leap and swing around structures in ways that really shouldn't have worked. Parking structures were especially cohesive to her acrobatics, with short walls and open spaces at every turn.

On the street, she whispered a thank you to whoever was listening for a clear path across. After a quick assessment of the scene, she grabbed Tyler Jacobson by both arms. She wanted to separate the bodies as much as possible, as she hoped the younger one was still alive following the blow to his head. She dragged Tyler Jacobson as far down the alley as she thought was safe. Then, with the containment collar in place, she went back to the kid, stopping only long enough to check for a pulse. She pulled his phone from his pocket and dialed 911.

"Nine-one-one, what's your emergency?"

She considered acting like a panicky tourist but decided better of it, instead speaking calmly and matter-of-factly. "Some guy just hit another guy in the head with a hammer and took off. In an alley off Market Street, between Nineteenth and Twentieth."

She ended the call before the man on the other end could make her stay and help. Not with her crossbow on the roof across the street.

And she had left the door open on the SUV.

She wiped the phone's screen on the tail of her shirt and dropped it to the ground next to the kid.

Back on the roof of the garage, with her weapon loaded into the guitar case, she pounded her fists against the steering wheel of the 1970s model SUV, screaming a string of swears into the cabin around her. "What the fuck is your deal? Why can't you get anything right?" she asked the pale face in the rearview mirror. The pale face in the mirror offered no response, and Fia jerked the key in the ignition.

She let the car lead the way, and together they found a bar she had checked out a couple of times. It was a college bar, but the clientele belonged more to the state college than one of the universities. The university clientele was khakis and button-downs—Brent Newmans. This was a t-shirts-and-jeans crowd. Her kind of crowd. She pulled the car into a nearby parking lot, locked up, and walked the block and a half to the bar, flashing her ID to the girl at the door and dropping a five in the jar.

There was a small stage opposite the bar, but there had been someone on it only one time she had been in there. It really wasn't a concert venue. She took a seat at the bar and ordered a shot of whiskey.

Maybe she was just off her game. Alan Chambers never should have gotten the jump on her the way he had. Her mind had been on that creepy priest and his no-neck thug drawing the drunk guy toward the church despite the drunk guy trying to take a chunk out of no-neck's shoulder.

She had thought, at first glance, the "drunk guy" had been several sheets to the wind, but the more she had watched and the more she thought about it, the less convinced she was. She couldn't nail down precisely why, but even from fifty yards away, she had gotten a weird feeling off him.

She held the shot glass up in front of her face, looking through the amber liquid at her reflection in the mirror at the back of the bar, before tossing it back. The bartender pantomimed pouring her another, and she shook her head. "Maybe just a cola." He nodded and drew a soda from the tap. "Cherry?" He winked and plopped two maraschinos into her glass, holding her gaze until the eye contact reached the point of too much. She rolled her eyes and shook her head. "Just here for the cola, thanks."

She pulled one of the cherries from its stem with her fingers instead of her teeth, refusing to encourage him any more than he thought she had already. She took a long drink from the glass, eschewing the straw for the same reason.

She lost time, focusing on her drink and the unusual events of the past few days. When she looked up again, the bar had started to fill up. A different bartender, female this time, set a glass in front of her.

"What's this?"

"Whiskey and cola. From him." The bartender pointed a short, stubby finger at a guy sitting a few stools down.

Fia recognized him. It had been a couple of months, probably, but she had taken him home from this same bar.

Aaron? Adam? Yeah, Adam. She was 98 percent certain . . . 95 percent certain it was Adam.

She was selfish; she took guys like him back to her apartment to get her off. Sometimes they didn't even make it as far as the apartment. Sometimes it was mutual, and sometimes she wrapped her legs around their necks and then sent them packing.

She knew she was selfish, but this guy had put that to shame. He had been a yo-yo. She had pushed him down; he had come right back up. "I ain't gonna end up jerking it over some dirty slut," he had said, pulling on her legs to get her to lie flat.

With a swift kangaroo kick to his chest, she had thrown him to the floor, gotten up, and held open the front door. "Don't know what to tell you, then, bro, because you're done here."

He had put on a good show, like he thought he was

going to intimidate her. In the end, though, getting tossed like a doll by a girl half his size had probably been embarrassing enough for him to not want to try again, and he had complied, leaving her alone in the apartment.

Now he was trying to buy her a drink? She flashed him an intentionally fake smile and, maintaining eye contact, nudged the glass back toward the bartender. "Tell him, 'No, thanks.'" She exaggerated the shape of "No, thanks" so he would get the message twice. Then she returned her attention to her cola.

It wasn't long before the energy around her shifted, and his presence was undeniable. He smelled of cheap cologne, even cheaper beer, and pheromones.

"Hey, gorgeous, don't you remember me?"

Fia tossed back the remainder of her cola, spitting a stray ice cube back into the glass. She scooted the glass to the rubber mat on the back edge of the bar, tucking a twenty-dollar bill beneath it for both her drinks and tip. She gave the female bartender a wave to let her know she was paid and leaving. Then she pushed around the creeper who couldn't take a hint, without acknowledging his question.

He wasn't tall, but she thought maybe he had been before something heavy fell on his head and compacted his frame into something wider than it should have been. She thought it would take an act of God to make him do something he didn't want to do.

Like stay put. She was aware of him following her out the door and stopped on the sidewalk a few yards from the bouncer guarding the front door. She could take care of herself, but it never hurt to have backup, especially against an opponent two of her across.

"What?" She spat the word as if it were the pit of one of her cherries.

"I guess you didn't hear me inside, eh, beautiful? I asked if you remember me. We had a good time a month or so ago. Thought you might want an encore."

"No, I remember you fine, and I remember kicking your selfish ass to the curb. Why would I want an encore of that?"

He stepped forward and put a hand on her hip, pulling her into his pelvis. "That ain't how I remember it."

She rolled her eyes and pried herself free of his grip. "You're something special, for sure. I'm going home. Alone. If you try to follow me, you'll be buying your next drink through your fly."

She turned to head back to the Scout. With reflexes she didn't expect from someone his size, he grabbed her scarred wrist and dragged back on it hard enough to make her gasp.

"I suggest you let go of me. Immediately, if not sooner," she growled.

He responded by pulling harder, twisting her to face him.

"I believe the lady asked you to let her go."

Fia snapped her head in the direction of the voice, expecting to see the bouncer, but the commanding baritone belonged to a man half Adam's size. The drummer. Coming in from the other side of the street.

"Where did you come—you know what? Never mind. I've got it under control."

"You heard the lady." The human cube gave the words *the lady* an extra mocking syllable. "She's got it under control. So scram, kiddo."

Fia thought the drummer was going to back off—until Adam's *kiddo* crack. The next crack she heard was bone on bone as the little drummer's fist connected with her assailant's jaw.

"You've had it now, shrimp." Adam released Fia's arm and grabbed the drummer by the shirt, slamming him into the bricks and punching him in the gut with his other hand. He swung again, this time aiming higher and connecting with the drummer's mouth.

While his advances on Fia had been subtle and small, this scuffle caught the bouncer's attention, and before Adam could land his third punch, the bouncer was pulling the two men apart.

He held Adam at arm's length, his gorilla paws wrapped around Adam's bicep, and turned to face the smaller of the two men, Fia's accidental Galahad. "You okay, bro?"

The drummer wiped blood from his mouth, looking at the red streak on the back of his hand. "Yeah, EJ, man, I'm good."

EJ turned back to Adam and gave him a shove. "I don't want to see you back here tonight. Get lost."

"I gotta get back inside and pay for my drinks."

"What're you drinking? I'll let 'em know you're not coming back for them. Get. Lost." Adam opened his mouth to attempt another ploy to get back inside, but EJ shut him down. "Go. Away. Or I'm calling the cops."

"Cops ain't gonna do nothing. I ain't doing nothing but having a drink and tryna get this hot little honey to go home with me."

EJ turned to face Fia this time. "Your turn. You wanna hit him? I'll give you a pass."

She shook her head. "I really just want to go home."

"I think you got lucky tonight, asshole. Now blow." EJ gave Adam a final nudge toward the parking lot.

Adam took a threatening step toward the drummer, blew Fia a kiss, and flipped EJ both middle fingers before sulking off toward the parking lot.

"Kind of a shame, really," EJ said as he watched to make sure Adam didn't double back but actually found a car in the lot.

"How's that?" the drummer asked, still dabbing at his swollen and split lip. Fia was inching back away from the situation, hoping to disappear while the other two men were distracted.

"I was looking forward to seeing her beat the tar out of him." EJ turned back to Fia. "Seriously, though? You good?"

She put up her hands, examining the drummer out of the corner of her eye. EJ had stepped in before Adam could do any real damage, but his lip was split open, blood was starting to surface in the creases of his knuckles, and his watering eyes spoiled his attempts at hiding his pain.

"Yeah, I'm golden. Can I go?"

EJ nodded. "Be careful, eh? You look like a tough chick, but he was three times your size."

She returned the nod. "Yeah, I'll . . . keep that in mind. Thanks."

She looked at the drummer. *If that Neanderthal was three times your size, he was easily twice the drummer's size, but he still stepped in to defend you. Maybe say thank you?*

"And you? Thank you. But don't follow me." She backed down the sidewalk a few more steps before pivoting toward where she had left the Scout.

Thirteen

Seven years earlier . . .

The intoxicating scent of pit-smoked meat filled the cold winter air behind Billy Boy's BBQ, where Fia sat on a low concrete wall waiting for the owner. Zeke leaned against the wall beside her, and another kid from their camp stood a few feet away.

As Billy stepped through the back door holding four white foam to-go boxes, Fia regarded the steam rising from the containers with appreciation. The leftovers from Billy Boy's BBQ were always great, hot or cold, but today Fia was grateful they were hot.

Billy had been bringing out boxes the health department said needed to be thrown away for long enough, it was one of the first things Fia had learned when she found the teens' homeless camp:

Keep your hands to yourself.

No drugs in camp.

Billy gives away barbecue at 3 p.m. on Sundays and Wednesdays.

It was a quiet time for him, between lunch and dinner, and he was usually alone in the tiny shack.

Fia wiped unapologetically at the corners of her mouth, anticipating what she would find when she opened the container she and Zeke would share. Knowing what she had stashed in the couch back at the warehouse, she felt a pang of guilt for taking the free leftovers from Billy.

Though maybe he'd get in trouble with the health department if he accepted money for it.

It made sense, but it didn't make her feel any better. She vowed to bring him one of those fifties the next time they came back. Even if she had to slip it under the door after he thought they had left.

"Hey, kids. Sorry I ain't got much for ya today. Been swamped."

Billy was a transplant from the South. The Deep South. And he looked and sounded every bit the part. He was a small man, rail thin, and his collarbones showed like he himself hadn't been getting enough to eat. Closely shorn white hair stood in stark contrast against his dark skin, permanently tanned from spending his youth in the sun. He wore a white cotton apron, stained with barbecue sauce, over a white t-shirt and loosely fitting blue jeans with white canvas sneakers. Fia didn't think she had seen him in anything else in the few months she had been coming here.

Billy extended the boxes to the teens. The other boy grabbed one off the top and dove in greedily, muttering a garbled thanks.

"Yeah, thanks, Billy." Fia took the other three boxes off his hands, the warm leftovers soothing her tingling fingers. One thing she hadn't considered when she struck out on her own was how cold this city could be in the winter.

Or how deeply she hated being cold.

Anyone who showed up at the designated time split whatever Billy had to give them. Fia and Zeke always shared a box. Because it was just the three of them today, Fia offered a second box to the other kid—Caleb, maybe, or Carter? She was fairly sure it was a Ca- name.

"Have you seen Poe?" she asked Zeke after the other kid had accepted the box and taken off back toward the camp.

"Not for a couple days. Honestly, not much since you two . . ." He left the sentence hanging in the thin icy air.

Besides Zeke, Poe McGinty was one of the first people Fia had met after leaving the convent. Zeke had gotten her off the streets and into the warehouse. Poe had gotten her into a job waiting tables at a diner, a situation that had unfortunately ended badly for both of them. Poe came into the camp on and off. Parker, Poe's twin, had a way of finding other places to stay.

"Guess one for each of us, then?"

Zeke shrugged. "Sure."

Fia had gone home after the incident with Mr. No Means Yes and hadn't left the apartment the entire next day. Instead, she had slept, most of it a dreamless, heavy sleep, not realizing how exhausting everything running off the rails had been. She had gotten up only long enough to eat dinner and then fallen asleep again on the couch.

Now it was day two with nothing to keep her busy, and she struck out early while the sun was still low over the plains, taking the Scout for a drive along the back roads to the southwest of the city. She tooled through the mountains, alternating between paved two-lane roads and rough dirt roads, enjoying the chance to see foliage arranged in a different pattern and trees she wasn't so used to. After all the trips to the bunker, she wasn't convinced she couldn't find a specific tree if she needed to.

The idea had been to clear her mind, to think about nothing but the smell of nutrient-rich soil and spruce trees for a few hours, but that had been less than successful. Instead, her memories had flooded with people from a different part of her life. Memories of Zeke, the McGinty twins, people she had known in the homeless camp where she had spent a large portion of two years.

After driving aimlessly and losing track of nearly four hours, Fia found her way back to the interstate highway, north to downtown. She parked in a garage and hoofed it the rest of the way, about six quiet blocks, to the place her memories were guiding her to.

Even after she no longer needed the kindness, Billy Boy's BBQ remained one of Fia's favorite places. The restaurant was a shack, really, not even as big as her condo. Most of Billy's business was takeout, though he did have room for sixteen people to dine in at four tables. It was informal, order and pick up at the counter. During the lunch and dinner times, he'd have two extra people—one in the kitchen and one doing basically everything else. From two until four in the afternoon, Billy took care of everything alone, and anyone who wandered through just had to accept that.

A collection of Christmas bells signaled Fia's arrival, and she strode up to the counter to wait for the leather-skinned man with silver-white hair to step out from the back.

"Miz Fia!" Despite having lived in the far-west edge of the Midwest for three decades, Billy still sounded like his pit-smoked barbecue smelled.

Smoky and deeply southern.

"What can I do ya for today, Miz Fia?"

"Chopped pork, Billy."

"Ya got it. Comin' right up."

He disappeared into the back, and she found a table in the corner, busying herself with her phone while she waited. She was lost deep in thought when Billy took the seat across from her, setting her box on the table between them. He had upgraded from foam to paper containers, but he still served everything in to-go boxes, regardless. It was just part of the atmosphere.

"Miz Fia, is somethin' the matter?"

"Huh?" She studied his face, momentarily forgetting where she was. "Oh, yeah. No, I mean, just work stuff."

"I hear a lotta that in here, for sure. Lotta people workin' in these buildin's round here comin' in lookin' for quiet away from their work stuff." He nudged the box closer to her. "Y'enjoy this one on me."

"I couldn't. I mean, it's not that kind of work stuff."

"I insist, Miz Fia. Ya got y'self offa the streets and keep comin' back for mah 'cue. I feel I owe ya for that."

"Okay. But only because I don't think I'm going to change your mind."

He grinned, stood up from the table, and leaned over to kiss her head. "I dunno what it is ya do, Miz Fia, but seems like y'doin' pretty fine for bein' a street kid."

He shuffled off to the back, and she dug into the box of smoky pork. Over the years, he'd figured out how she liked it and always made her box just right: with his home-made bourbon sauce in a cup on the side. She scooped up a forkful of the dark red meat and dipped it gently into the cup. She loved the sauce, but the meat was good enough on its own, and she didn't like to mask that.

She finished as quickly and quietly as she could, hoping

to slip out before he returned to the front. He was probably busy washing dishes or still preparing boxes for the kids in the area. Her camp had been paved over a few years before, but there were still kids. Kids who had lit out from farther east, thinking they were going to LA or Portland to become famous, but who got stuck halfway. Kids who had run away from abusive foster homes to avoid being placed somewhere worse. Kids who had simply aged out of the foster care system and had nowhere to go when they did.

She reached across the counter and tucked a fifty-dollar bill under the front edge of the cash register. "Thanks for lunch, Billy," she called into the kitchen.

"Sure thang!"

The size of the shack where Billy served his legendary barbecue didn't really allow for the subarctic temperatures most restaurants kept during the summer, so stepping back into the summer heat wasn't quite the shock it normally would have been. Fia stretched her neck and shoulders, soaking up the rays of sunlight beating down on them, and started back toward where she had left the Scout.

She had put a block between herself and the smell of barbecue when she saw him. The priest. Father Creepy. His rigid posture was unmistakable. Something in the way he watched her made her feel like he had been waiting for her to come out of the restaurant. She stopped and met his gaze from the opposite side of the street, holding it, predator to predator, challenging him to do whatever he was going to do.

But instead of taking her challenge and approaching her, he turned and retreated up a side street. He was headed for the cathedral, she guessed. Having nothing else to do but go back to her apartment and count the air bubbles in the bricks, Fia chose to follow him. She crossed against the light, not wanting to waste any time catching up to him and not feeling like she needed to hide the fact she was tailing him. She had a fairly good idea that he wanted her to.

The cathedral was a block east and another south. It was a conspicuous Gothic relic, tiny in comparison to the office buildings that had grown up around it, beautiful for all its buttresses and carvings. The warm cream-colored sandstone was a stark contrast to the mirrored glass of the surrounding skyscrapers.

She was still half a block behind the priest when he entered the cathedral through a side door that was only slightly less ornate than the main doors leading into the sanctuary.

As she prepared to cross the street, still a considerable distance from the church, he stepped out again. He ushered a nun through the door ahead of him, his hand on the small of her back. Fia quickly ducked behind a parked car, situating herself so she could see through the windows, giving her full privilege to the scene as it unfolded, though her view of any identifying features was obscured.

The nun turned and faced the priest, the heavy edges of her robe moving slowly around her body. Both looked around in every direction imaginable before turning back to one another. The priest leaned down, meeting the nun at her level as he pushed her hair behind her shoulders. Fia strained to determine if he was merely speaking quietly into her ear or if the action was deeper, but he drew back before she could decide. The nun handed her veil over to the priest, quickly twisted her thick hair into a braid that stretched nearly to her waist before tucking it into the collar of her robe, and slipped the veil into its proper place.

Even from this distance, Fia could feel the intensity with which the priest watched the young sister as she descended to the small parking lot and out into the street. There, a black sedan had just arrived, a magnetic rideshare logo affixed to the front door panel.

"Well, that's not something you see every day."

Fia looked around as they had to see if there had been anyone else nearby. There was no one on the street, but there was no guarantee someone hadn't been looking out one of the mirrored windows overhead. Fia thought the priest and nun had taken a pretty big risk by not saying what looked like inappropriately intimate goodbyes while still hidden behind the door.

Though maybe it was a show for Fia. She was sure the priest had known she was following him. But what kind of show? He may have whispered in the nun's ear; he may have kissed her cheek. It had been impossible to determine from this distance. If the priest had wanted Fia to see . . . something, then she had missed the point.

She waited for him to go back inside before following the rest of the way. She decided that what she had just seen would stay her little secret until she needed a card to play. Even though she had only seen him at a distance these few times, it was a few times too many for her having never seen him before, and there was something about him that was just creepy. Not counting the incident with the zombie in the mall, between the first time Fia had seen him and again today, she was certain he was following her. And the only way she knew to find out why was to confront him and ask.

The first time she had seen the priest, he had gotten into a car with a woman at the wheel. Fia hadn't gotten a good look at the driver's face, but she had seen enough of the woman's ponytail and this nun's thick braid to make a confident wager they were the same person.

Fia crossed the street after giving the priest a few

seconds on the other side of the door. Though smaller than the sanctuary doors at street side, this side door was still larger than a standard door, crafted from solid wood and brass hardware, and it looked heavy. She pulled at it, expecting it to weigh as much as a small car, and nearly fell over backward when it didn't.

Inside, the church smelled like a church: dust, vanillin, linseed oil, and stale air. Despite three large windows that faced the parking lot outside, the hallway was dark and left Fia blinking furiously to adjust to the lack of light. The stale air clinging to her was cool, almost cold. She rubbed at her arms to ease the intensity of the new sensation.

Once she could see, she looked up and down the hallway, trying to figure out where the priest had gone. As she looked to her left, he stepped out of the shadows at her right elbow.

"Is there something I can help you with?" He spoke with a drawl that sounded like it had been filtered through broken glass.

Fia took a step away from him as she turned. She met his eyes, black in the dim light, and committed to memory the deep hollows between his sharp cheekbones and sharp jaw. She thought back to the description Zeke had given her of the man who had left her first bounties.

Tall. Taller than me, lanky, all arms and legs. Mostly unexceptional. And his nose. More of a beak than a nose.

This was not that man. Zeke had been over six feet tall by two or three inches. This man standing in front of Fia now had a few inches to go before he even reached six feet. And he had an average-looking nose, despite all the other harsh angles that made up his face.

She weighed her options: ask him why he was following her, point blank, or see if she could get him to hang himself.

Standing this close to him, the uneasy feeling she had had from several hundred feet away had intensified exponentially, and she had no doubt he had been following her. She fought back the urge to clutch her churning gut.

"Just thought I'd have a look around. Pretty place you've got here." The lie felt feeble, but maybe that was better. Let him in on the ruse. Make him wonder why she was lying.

After all, it wasn't like he didn't know that she knew he had been following her. He had acknowledged her twice.

What she really wanted to know was what had been wrong with the man she had seen him with in the mall. She wasn't ready to ask that question yet, though. She had to keep a few cards close to her vest, and as far as she knew, he hadn't seen her in the mall that afternoon.

The priest smiled with only his teeth, none of the expression reaching his dark eyes. "Yes, it is. One of the first buildings in this part of the city, after it became a city."

"Sure."

"Unchanged, in many ways. Of course, some upgrades have been made. Air conditioning, speakers in the sanctuary."

"Electricity," Fia offered, playing along.

"Ah, yes, electricity. Very astute, Miss Drake." She bit back a reaction, maintaining what she hoped was a solid poker face. He knew her name!

Of course he does. Why else would he be following you?

"Not really. Kind of need electricity for speakers. I'm a bit of an audiophile, kind of know my way around a speaker. At least, how to plug one in."

"Ah, of course." She could hear him breathing as he took a step closer to her. The twisted knot in her center tightened, but she held her stance. "Well, if you would like me to show you around . . ." He took another half step forward.

She took a deliberate breath, deep into her diaphragm, to mask her discomfort. Twice this month, she had found herself in close quarters with men who had gotten too close for comfort and wrapped their hands around her throat. She had no interest in a third go, but she hadn't gotten a good line on the priest's goals yet, and she wanted to try to figure him out, calmly, quietly. If he would allow it.

"I guess I have a little time for a tour."

She fell in half a step behind him, listening to his voice more than his words. She watched his body language as he expounded the historical relevance of this Victorian-era structure that was "small in comparison to its contemporaries, but still quite an undertaking—I'm certain an intelligent girl like you can imagine—without the aid of heavy equipment."

Intelligent girl *like you* . . . The words were complimentary; the tone and subtle influence he had put on "girl" were not.

What Fia didn't know was whether it was indicative of his general opinion of women or if she was just special.

She also wondered if this tour-guide routine was his regular priest persona or if it, too, was customized for her benefit. In the cavernous hall of the main sanctuary, as yellow light pouring through a section of stained glass jaundiced his face, she gave up her end of the act.

"Tell me, Father, do you do a lot of church-related business in Capitol Hill?" Even as she asked, she knew there was no reason he would have been in the area where she had first seen him, at the time she had seen him, to do business.

"I have had occasion to visit the area, to obtain permits for various events, you understand. But recently, I cannot say that I have. No, not in a fair time." The formality of his words—"had occasion to visit," "not in a fair time"— sounded to Fia like the wrong note being played in a familiar piece of music, an F where a G should be.

Not to mention the blatant lie. He hadn't taken the specific bait she had put out for him, but he had still lied, just as she had hoped he would.

"So that wasn't you I saw the other day . . . ?" She chose her next words carefully now, hoping to bait him into showing his own cards. "Outside the land offices? It was a day or two after they found those girls in the forest."

He curled his lip in a wolfish sneer. Fia's nerves lit up as her fight or flight instincts were triggered by the predatory expression, leaning more toward flight in that moment of uncertainty. She imagined the garter holster hidden beneath her cargo-style pants tightening around her thigh, reminding her that if push came to shove, she had a weapon.

But he had the house advantage.

And a thug with no neck who might or might not have been lurking in the shadows, waiting for her to make a move.

"Ah, yes, Miss Drake, you are correct. I had forgotten about that day. I was obtaining a permit to have our teen group do a trash cleanup in one of the parks."

Bullshit. Since when do you need a permit to pick up litter?

"I see. I just . . . wondered where I might have seen you before." She took a quick glance at her phone, which showed nothing of importance, cooking up her own lie. "I am afraid I must call an end to our tour . . . educational as it has been. I need to get to another appointment."

"Of course. Come back again if you would like to learn more."

Was that part of the act, or was he now trying to bait her? "Thank you. I will." She decided that would sound good, no matter what his angle was. If he was simply drifting back into character, then it sounded like a pleasant formality. If he was trying to bait her, it sounded like she wasn't bothered by his veiled threats.

She took a step back the way they had come, then a step toward the main doors. "Uh, which way should I—"

"You are welcome to leave the way you came in. I have some work to do in here. I trust you can see your way out?"

Fia nodded and retreated to the side hallway. As she rounded the corner into the dimly lit corridor, movement caught her eye.

About a hundred feet away, another older man had stepped out of an office and was taking a quick look up and down the hallway. He was dressed in a cassock, his white hair thin across his glossy pink scalp and his heavyset shoulders slightly hunched. His cheeks, which Fia guessed from the rest of his aesthetic should have been a deep salmon, were burning red, his light-colored eyes wide and nervous.

When Fia first saw him, she stepped back out of sight, pressed against the wall of a little area separating the sanctuary from the hallway. When this second priest seemed to find the coast clear, he scooted down the hall on disproportionately short legs and out the side door Fia had come in, out into the summer heat.

She followed a few seconds later. Anonymity, or invisibility, seemed important to him, so Fia let him have it. She didn't follow him intentionally, but casually waited to see which direction he went before continuing toward her car in the garage a couple of blocks away.

In her pocket, her phone emitted the cheeky *cha-ching* of the drop box's motion sensor.

FOURTEEN

arshall Wallace owned several elaborate, expensive boutique hotels in the city, each designed around a gemstone: the Sapphire, Ruby, and Emerald Houses. According to his file, some of his guests were checking in but never checking out. Or rather, as the song suggests, they checked out, but they never left.

Tourists made easy prey. No one was expecting them to walk in the front door that night, and the horrors that might befall them on their journey were innumerable. From fake taxi abductions to plane crashes, it was not unheard of for vacationers to never return home. And because the people at home expected them to be gone, out of touch as they enjoyed their trip, their absence wasn't felt until they didn't return to work for their scheduled shifts.

Tourists made easy prey, and Marshall Wallace was preying on them.

Sometimes Fia wondered if the violent, malevolent souls she was hunting would have even stood out in their original forms in modern times. How truly atrocious could someone be with a knife, compared to guns and bombs? At the same time, though, stabbing one's spouse and children forty-seven times in their sleep was probably worse than being completely disconnected from the people being blown up in a train station.

Perspective.

Down in the bunker, Fia packed up a few things—camera, GPS trackers—threw on a light shirt with a hood and dark sunglasses, and headed back to the surface to try to find murderous hotelier Marshall Wallace.

The Sapphire House was gawdy, even by boutique standards. Fia never could understand why people spent money on things like this or why they expected them to look like this if they did. The granite-tiled floor alone had probably reduced some mountain somewhere to a molehill. It was white, mostly, with veins of gray, black, and real, raw gold.

Every overwrought mahogany Queen Anne chair in the lobby was upholstered in the same deep-blue velvet fabric. There were gold silk throw pillows on the matching sofas, and crystal-and-gold chandeliers hung every fifty feet or so, providing none of the actual light in the giant open space. The doors of the two elevators were gold, bright, shiny yellow and polished to a mirror finish, without a fingerprint in sight. The staff were all decorated in the same blue-and-gold silk. Starched black shirts and pressed black slacks that were likely maintained by the hotel laundry were accented by blue vests and gold bowties, men and women alike.

The difference between the tourists and the business travelers roaming through the lobby was stark. While tourists came in touting everything they owned, men and women in expensive suits checked in carrying little more than an oversize briefcase, some with garment bags slung over one shoulder. Tourists struggled to maneuver eight suitcases and five people into one elevator, while the business travelers left their minimal belongings with the hotel porter.

In her worn jeans and hooded t-shirt, Fia looked more like the tourists. She watched as several of each filtered past the front desk, waiting, possibly in vain, for Marshall Wallace to show.

Just as she was ready to give up on hour four of her stakeout—having spent the whole day bouncing from a chair in the lobby to a stool in the lounge to the bus bench across the street to avoid being accused of loitering—her target emerged from an office behind the front desk. She let him find his way out of the hotel into the street before following him.

Marshall Wallace was young, for all he had accomplished. Fia thought it was a little tragic that someone so young—thirty-five, according to his dossier—who had accomplished so much was now effectively dead and being animated by a condemned soul that would use his corpse until it deteriorated enough to be unusable and then leave it to rot in an alley.

She followed him five blocks to another of his properties—the Ruby, which was decorated similarly to the Sapphire, but with red in place of the blue—hanging back far enough to determine where he went once he was inside. If he was here to camp out in his office for another four hours, she might just call it a day. She felt lucky that no one at the first property had hassled her for loitering; she didn't want to push that luck and risk her cover, tenuous as it already was.

It was with relief, then, that she watched him slip into the restaurant. Realizing the sandwich she had eaten earlier had been replaced with an angry rumbling, she continued the pursuit of her target.

Even as guests were checking into the hotel, the restaurant dining room remained sparsely populated at three in the afternoon. Marshall Wallace breezed past the host stand and took a seat at a table near the front; Fia guessed it was his exclusive reserved seat. She slipped a twenty to the maître d' and asked for a table near the door. "I'm waiting for a blind date," she explained. "Might need an easy escape route."

She fell into her usual routine, watching her target to see how long he might be staying. Since Marshall Wallace had a reserved table, he probably wouldn't need to consult a menu before ordering. Which meant that stalling was off her itinerary. She took a chance on the bruschetta, deciding if she needed to stall longer, she could always order something else.

With one eye on her phone to look distracted and the other on her target, Fia watched the eccentric hotelier swirl his wine around the edges of the glass, sniffing at it before taking a sip, which he swirled in his mouth and spit back into the glass.

Fia was thankful no one had properly taught her to waste her money. She was content with the warm burn of cheap whiskey. When they were sixteen and screwing in the back of Rylan's muscle car, she and Rylan had been drinking the best he could pay the mechanic he worked for to buy, which had still been cheap. She had upgraded some, but not to the point of swish and spit.

Marshall Wallace placed an order from memory. Since the tomatoes and cheese of the bruschetta were doing very little to quell the complaints from her gut, Fia took another gamble on a hot sandwich. Afterward, the waitress returned with a bowl of soup for her employer, and Fia cursed under her breath.

"All this work, and I'm going to lose this son of a bitch over a sandwich."

Eager not to let that happen, she all but inhaled the sandwich, managing all but a few bites before Marshall Wallace signed his check. She did a quick bit of math in her head and tossed a fifty-dollar bill on the table to cover her check and tip, slightly disgusted by what people were willing to pay for so little. She fell into step behind the man as he headed north toward the entertainment district, which she knew like her own name.

As they came closer to the blocks surrounding the professional baseball field in the heart of downtown, the foot traffic increased and the vehicle traffic waned considerably. On game days, the city blocked off the streets, two blocks in every direction, to keep pedestrian-involved accidents to a minimum. It resulted in something that resembled Mardi Gras—purple t-shirts replacing strings of beads and ball caps in place of feathered masks.

In the dense crowd, Marshall Wallace was easily able to slip his tail, whether he meant to or not. This was one case, Fia thought, that truly demonstrated the control exerted over the host by the soul inside. Alive, she didn't think an agoraphobic eccentric like Marshall Wallace would have been caught dead in this kind of crowd.

Or anywhere near baseball fans.

Fia slipped into a quiet-looking pub to assess the situation, regroup, and decide on her next step. She took a seat at the bar and ordered a cola. The place was quiet, despite the mob outside. She could hear shouts of revelry drifting in through the open door—the game must have gone well.

"You don't benefit much from the game crowd?" she asked the bartender, a tough-looking woman in a black t-shirt advertising an old country singer from decades past. Her salt-and-pepper hair was pulled into a high, no-frills ponytail, and her deeply leathered skin implied years working outdoors before moving inside to peddle booze.

"Nah, they're looking for more action than I've got to offer." She waved a long, bony hand vaguely around the room. "I ain't even got a jukebox."

"What she lacks in entertainment, though, she makes up for in good whiskey. Hey, Kate."

"Hey, Max. The usual?" The leathered bartender pulled a bottle Fia didn't recognize down from a high shelf.

"For me. And add hers to my tab."

Fia turned to face the speaker, though she didn't need to see his face to know who was trying to buy her drinks; that heavy, rich baritone had already cemented itself in her memory. She hadn't met too many men of his slight stature who had a voice that sounded like it originated near the core of the earth. It was hard to forget. Just the same, she turned toward his cheeky smile and intense brown stare.

"No. Don't put mine on his tab. In fact—" She downed the last of her cola and stepped down from her stool, pushing the glass back to Kate. "I've had enough. I'm going home." She pulled out a stack of cash—what was left from breaking a fifty earlier in the day—and reached to hand Kate a ten.

"Please," the drummer said, stepping in front of her.

Damn, he smells good.

Fia moved to step around him, only to have him zig as she zagged. "What?" she snapped, more harshly than she had meant to. She dialed it back, though not enough to sound nice. "What do you want?"

"I'd like to talk."

"Is that why you've been following me? Look, I don't know what I did or said—"

"I'm not following you."

"You're here. You charged in the other night on your white horse to save me from that meathead and his meat hooks. Explain that if you aren't following me."

"Coincidence." It wasn't a question. The drummer offered the answer with all the confidence in the world.

"Coincidence? You expect me to believe that?"

"I don't expect anything. I'm actually surprised we haven't met before; I get the impression we have a lot of the same hobbies."

"Hobbies?"

"Well, bars and music, anyway."

Fia cocked an eyebrow at him. "Are you calling me—"

"No! I'm not calling—hey, look, we had a good time. At least, I had a good time, and you sounded like you were having a good time. I got the impression you weren't looking for anything . . . but I kind of . . . can I please buy you a drink and at least find out your first name? I feel like we're bound to run into each other again."

Fia studied his face for a long moment. All the voices of reason in her brain were screaming at her to walk away. But every one of her nerve endings, especially the ones responsible for pleasure, were urging her to give him a chance to say what he had to say. *That good smell? Pheromones. He smells like hot sex.*

"Fine. *One* drink. Say what you have to say before I finish it."

She started climbing back up onto the stool, but he pulled her by the hand, guiding her toward a table near the back of the room, as far as they could get from the open door without sitting in the restroom.

"It's quieter back here." He pulled a chair out for her, waiting for her to sit before pushing her closer to the table. "What am I getting you?"

"What was that bottle she pulled down for you?"

"Local batch. Good stuff. You like whiskey?" He was practically drooling, so she said she did. "Neat? You can mix it, but—"

"Neat is fine."

He returned to the bar to pick up the glass Kate had already poured for him and ask her for a second one. She shook her head, an amused smirk curling one side of her thin lips. "The Max Hawkins charm strikes again," she said, almost laughing. "Why don't you have a full-time, kid?"

"They can't handle the rock-star life, Kate."

"Shame." She pushed Fia's glass over to him and returned her attention to a sink full of dirties.

He set Fia's drink in front of her and took the seat across the table. "I'm Max. I don't think we ever got to that point."

"We didn't. Or . . . I didn't." She reached out her scarred right hand to shake his, watching his eyes now that he had a calm moment to register what he was looking at. He shook her hand without flinching, gripping it with the same gentle firmness he had once applied to her thighs before returning it to her. "I actively avoid exchanging names. It's usually easier that way. Makes it harder for people to ask around about me."

His eyebrows furrowed together, and he sucked his teeth. "You really are a hard nut to crack, aren't you?"

"I try to be."

"Why?"

That she could answer, without bringing him into a world where mythical birds interrupted one-night stands. "Because the world sucks and it's easier if you don't let people get too close."

"Can I at least call you something? How about Red?"

"Please don't. Name's Fia."

"Fia. It fits. Sounds fiery."

"Fiammetta is what the government calls me. It means *little flame.*"

He tilted his head to the side, curling a corner of his full lips into a thoughtful smile. "Did your parents know you were going to be . . . ?" He reached out and twisted one of the longer strands of her short hair between his fingers.

"I don't know. Maybe. Didn't know my parents." She punctuated the statement with a dismissive shrug and a sip of the amber liquid in her glass.

Max straightened up in his chair, visibly startled by her confession. If she were being honest, she was a little startled by it as well. "Wow. Sorry. I didn't mean—"

"I mean, I've had a couple decades to come to terms with it. It's not like you're rubbing salt in a fresh wound. The scars have healed."

"Still . . . I'm going to cut to the chase, Fia—"

"Probably best, considering you only have until I finish my drink, remember?"

He nodded to her glass. "You like it? It's smooth, yeah?"

"It's good."

"Good? It's great. I think it's the mountain spring water."

"They say that about the beer here too."

He laughed. "That's fair." He took another deep pull

from his glass, holding her eyes over the top as he did. Then he put the glass down on the table. "Tell me about the bird."

"Bird?" she asked, confused. He dipped his chin, peering at her over the top of imaginary spectacles, like some disapproving schoolmarm. "Oh, *that* bird."

"There was more than one?"

"No, just the one. It's been a long month." She gulped at the whiskey—it was exceptional, but she wasn't ready to tell him that—and set the glass down. "Okay, you get a reprieve. I'll let you buy me one more, and *then* we're done."

He winked at her and hurried to the bar for another round before she could change her mind. Once he returned, he looked at her expectantly, waiting for her to start telling whatever story she was going to tell.

She wasn't fully sure which story he was going to get. She had no idea how to explain what he had seen—what *they* had seen—in her apartment. She was only certain *she* had seen it because he was bringing it up now.

"You want to know about the bird."

"I'd like to know a lot of things, but we can start with the bird."

"I'm still working on the bird."

The truth was, she had pushed it from her mind. At least, as far from her mind as possible when she had had a gaping hole in the side of her apartment. She had gotten that fixed, but between that creepy priest and his vaguely threatening demeanor and the mark who had tried strangling her before she got his fact sheet, the appearance of what could have, until thirty seconds ago, just as easily been a hallucination, had been the easiest thing to file away for deeper analysis at a later time.

Now, it was a later time.

And it hadn't been a hallucination.

"Working? On the bird?"

"Yeah. At least you knew what it was."

"You didn't?"

"I did, on some level. I just hadn't assembled my thoughts by the time you came in. But as far as where it came from, what it was doing in my apartment, how it burst through—as you astutely pointed out—bulletproof glass—none of that has revealed itself to me."

Max stroked a hand over his long chin but said nothing.

"You're taking this all really well."

"No sense in losing my mind until I figure out what I'm looking at." He paused. "Unless I should be losing my mind?"

"I think I am." He didn't respond, only held his eyes steady on hers. "Look, Max, I live a weird life. I live in a weird world—"

"With phoenixes."

"With phoenixes. And to be fair, that's new. I think it's probably best for everyone if you just cut your losses, chalk this up as something to tell your grandkids about one day, and forget you ever met me."

"I can't get you out of my head."

"Stop that. Immediately."

He kept talking as if she hadn't said anything. "You're captivating, for starters. Your attitude is so commanding. And you know what you want. I like that. Look, Fia, I'm not saying you don't have a weird life. I can see you have a weird life. Your weird life puts my weird life to shame. But for a guy like me to find a woman like you who can manage her shit . . . excuse me, but it's a little hard to walk away."

"A guy like you?"

"The music thing. It's different for someone who doesn't do it full-time or for people like Mitchell and Kim, who met before we got this thing off the ground. But a guy like me, who doesn't have any other real skills, who is dedicated to making music my life—I meet two kinds of girls: Girls who think they're going to live some glamorous life of luxury, only to find out that mostly it's just long hours locked up in the studio or in a van and a suffocating stench of body odor that happens no matter how much deodorant you wear. Or girls who want me to give it up. Stay home with them. Be Mr. Domestic. That's not me. I mean, I can wash my own shorts and keep myself fed, but I'm not looking to settle down with anyone anytime soon. I like the musician gig."

"And me?"

"I think, whatever you do, you do what you do with men—Men? People?—for the same reasons. You're into something that makes meaningful relationships a little impossible."

"There's that judgy tone again. You weren't so judgmental when you had your head—"

"I'm not judging you, Fia. That's what I'm trying to make you understand. I think we're kindred. There's something about both our lives—both our weird lives—that could make this mutually beneficial."

"This?"

"Whatever you want it to be. We could fuck. We could date. We could just be friends, because I think we could both use more. We could do all three."

Fia chewed on his words for a moment. "I don't think—you have proven already that just fucking isn't going to work for you. You're not programmed like that, Max. I can already see it. Just by dragging me into this conversation, you've proven you can't *just fuck*."

Without a word, Max stood up from the table and

started down the hallway toward what Fia assumed would be single-toilet restrooms at the back of the tiny bar. She heard the latch click closed and waited for another sound, the *click-clunk* of a dead bolt or slide lock. When she didn't hear any, she gave the bar a quick sweep to see if anyone was watching. Kate had disappeared from view, and the only other patrons were hunkered over a card game in the opposite corner.

Making her decision, Fia followed Max toward the restroom. She was halfway there when a scream of terror ripped through the air from the street outside.

FIFTEEN

The scream raised gooseflesh on Fia's arms. The men around the front table looked up from their card game, first at each other, then toward the pub's open door. Another scream followed, then another.

"You've got to be kidding me." Fia looked toward the restroom door and then back toward the street. Heaving a regretful sigh, she moved toward the front, grabbing her satchel from the floor on her way out.

Outside, she scanned the crowd, trying to determine where to start looking for the source of the screams. Another scream came from her left, and she spun toward it. The men who had been playing cards were on her heels.

"Get back inside and shut the door behind you," she hissed at them.

Two moved to follow her instructions but stopped when they noticed the other two hadn't.

"Now!" This time she shouted, putting every ounce of power she had into being as intimidating as she possibly could. She unfastened the flap of her pants where she had cut out the lining of the cargo pocket to create access to her garter sheath and pulled the blade free. It was only then that all four men took a step back, but they still didn't retreat inside.

She didn't actually know what she was going to do with the knife, but it had startled her tails enough that she lifted it toward them. They finally scuttled back inside, doing as she said and shutting the door behind them.

She flipped up the hood of her t-shirt, covering her hair and as much of her face as she could, and moved toward the last scream. There was no one on the raised walkway that ran along the front of the businesses. However, when she reached the next set of steps leading down to the lower sidewalk, she found a man at the bottom clutching uselessly at a gaping hole in his shoulder. Something had ripped enough flesh and muscle from his body that his hand was not enough to stop the bleeding.

"Call 911," she barked at a couple of gawking bystanders before moving farther down the street.

"Fia?"

She spun as someone grabbed her by the shoulder. Max had caught up to her. He must have heard the screaming from the restroom and followed her.

"Max! What the—get out of here! Or you know what, make yourself useful and see if you can help that guy."

"On it."

She didn't even have time to turn away before he took off his shirt, stuck two fingers into an already existing hole, and tore it in half. He had knelt beside the shocked and bleeding man and was setting to bandaging the wound when Fia returned to her pursuit. Back the way she had come, someone else screamed, the sound piercing the air like one of her bolts.

"Fia!" Max called after her, his voice cracking only slightly.

Well, that's better than nothing. At least something about this bothers him.

She moved back down the lower sidewalk in the direction Max had jerked his chin. On the other side of the bar, she found a small pack of onlookers who watched, slack-jawed, as a small, disheveled man gnashed his teeth at another larger man. The smaller of the two had, Fia guessed, pounced on the bigger man like a rabid animal, riding him to the ground. The bigger man was on his back, thrashing wildly. Every few swings, his thick, solid-looking arms would connect with the smaller man's face. The small man just kept snapping his jaws, spittle dripping from his dry, cracked lips.

Fia surveyed the scene. A quick count suggested twenty people were watching the horror show at her feet. *They're all in shock. There's a good chance they'll forget your face if you break this up.*

She tucked her knife into the belt loop at the back of her pants and grabbed the smaller man with both hands, hauling backward with all her weight, prepared to topple underneath him. Before that could happen, he turned on her, snapping his dripping jaws at her face.

It was then she caught the scent coming off him: like burned matches and a flooded basement no one had ever bothered to clean up. Sulfur and mildew. Death. The smell of matches was new, but that damp smell of mold was the same smell Alan Chambers had pressed into her nose and mouth with the palm of his hand.

Fia tried to get a good look at the man's eyes, but his movements were too erratic, too frantic, and she had to dodge his teeth at the same time.

"All right, McNasty, that's enough of that."

She drew back her arm and drove her fist into the soft area behind his jaw, under his ear. He reeled but didn't let up. The man who had been pinned beneath him regained his composure enough to help, pulling the smaller man off Fia and throwing him into the street.

The bigger man was big enough that the smaller one didn't simply slam into the asphalt in the closed-off street but slid a foot or two when he landed. Unfazed, he found his feet again, though a deep wound showed on his cheek. Fia thought the exposed underlayer of the wound was black, then decided it must be an illusion caused by the dim streetlamps. The man screeched, a sound reminiscent of the phoenix she had encountered only a few days earlier, and launched himself—teeth exposed, jaw working fervently— back into the crowd.

What is with this guy? What if it's just drugs? Molly? Didn't that make people bite each other?

Another voice in her head joined the first, the devil to her angel. *If you don't take him out, the cops will. What if he is possessed? A bullet to the head puts that soul into one of these bystanders. Are you ready for that?*

She secured her hood and grabbed the man, dragging him backward into her own space. In one fluid movement, she pulled the blade from her belt and sunk it into the man's spine.

"That's three," she muttered. Three she had taken out mano a mano. Three more that she had taken out by hand than she ever had before.

She deftly flipped the collar she had intended for Marshall Wallace from the pack slung across her torso and snapped it into place, letting the body fall where she dropped it. Then she turned to retreat, hopefully as unidentifiable as possible.

She could hear sirens coming. That collar would have someone here soon—*There is never one more than ten minutes away*—but not before the cops and EMS. She knew she was next to invisible with the hood, but she hadn't been when she snapped at those men in front of the bar.

She ducked into an alley and stripped out of the shirt, down to the tank top underneath. She stuffed the hooded t-shirt into her satchel—the satchel everyone in the crowd had seen—and peeked back out into the street. The man Max had patched up was an unfortunate shade of purple gray, but his eyes were open. The man who had tried to help her fight off the . . . whatever that was . . . looked bewildered but whole.

She scanned for Max, hoping to find him before he found her so she could avoid him.

No luck. He saw her half a second before she saw him. He gave a quick look left and right before hurrying toward her. She looked in the same directions he had, discovering what she thought had convinced him to head her way.

No one was looking at either of them, not directly. Pandemonium had set in. People were still screaming, crying. Fia noticed another victim she hadn't seen before, this one a woman who hadn't been as lucky as either man; the whole left side of her scalp and part of her skull was missing.

As Max caught up to her, Fia asked, "Did he *bite*—"

"What the *hell* just happened?"

"I think you nailed it."

"Huh?"

"Come on, I'll explain. Somewhere . . . somewhere else." She pulled him into the alley as the first of the response team pulled through the barricades into the crowded street.

She led him down the alley to the next block, looking

both ways before stepping out onto the sidewalk. "Act natural—shit."

Not only had Max left his shirt tied around the man's arm, he had blood splattered all over his pale chest. The sun had set while they were in the bar and they stood in deep shadows cast by the streetlamps, but there was no mistaking that that was blood on his chest. She pulled her shirt back out of her pack and handed it to him.

"I think it will fit. Do you have a car close by?"

He waved his hand back the way they had come. "I'll come back for it tomorrow."

"Probably for the best."

"Fia?"

"Yeah?"

"What was that?"

"A shitstorm." He met her eyes, his own gaze solid and flat. "Sorry. I think you were on the right track before. I think that was actual Hell. Gehenna. Abaddon. Call it what you want, I think that's what that was."

"Like, fire-and-brimstone, Satan, nine-circles Hell?"

"Kind of like, yes."

"I'm definitely going to need some explanation for that."

"Come on. We're not far from my place. You can get cleaned up and I'll tell you . . . something."

"That's promising."

"It's the best I got. I can't very well explain something I don't understand, can I?"

"I guess not."

"Come on."

This time, she led him straight to her apartment, which was, as she had said, only a few blocks from where they had started. She couldn't help watching the streetlights cross his face, trying to read his mind. The last few minutes had to have been a lot to process. A few days ago, he had thought he was in for a one-night stand, and now he was a willing accomplice after she had killed someone in front of him.

Not to mention the bird.

"Look—"

"Fia, I—"

Their words clashed, and they both fell silent again.

"Max," she tried again a minute later. "If you want, I can drive you back to your car and you can forge—"

"I liked that shirt. It was probably one of my favorites. Probably why it ripped so easy."

"What?"

"Nothing. Fia, look, I like you."

She wrinkled her face. "You like sex. You don't—"

"No. You're right. I don't know you. Not really. But I'd like to. You're captivating, exciting. Smart."

She stared at him, brow furrowed, mouth open. After all he had seen? What was the catch?

"You just watched me stab someone in the skull. You're covered in someone else's blood. I'm sorry about your shirt—"

She stopped, feeling her voice rising toward hysterical with every word. Nothing made any sense.

Max stayed quiet the rest of the way to the converted warehouses. When they got to the main door, he stopped, pulling her to face him.

"Here's what I do know. I know you are tough as hell, smart. You have a . . . well, your sense of humor is a lot like mine, which I'm not sure qualifies as great, but at least we can both laugh at inappropriate things together."

He paused, long enough for Fia to wonder if she was supposed to respond. With an inappropriate joke, perhaps?

"My timing is terrible," he finally continued.

"Huh?"

"Timing. We're leaving the day after tomorrow. For three weeks."

"Oh. Congratulations?"

"Yeah, thanks. No, I mean, that wasn't—" He sighed. "A national tour? I have never wanted anything more in my life."

"Sure."

"Except now, I want to just binge on everything Fia . . . Fia . . . starting with what comes after Fia."

She held his gaze for a moment before laughing. "I guess that would be a good place to start. Drake."

"Hawkins."

"Well, Max Hawkins, would you like to come upstairs and wash the stranger's blood off your chest?"

It was his turn to laugh. "Yes. If you don't mind."

She breathed a heavy sigh. "No. I think I might like the company."

As they crossed the brightly lit foyer, Fia let Max pull her against his side, wrapping her in a protective embrace. She savored the warm strength of his body, even as her rational mind screamed at her to step away. He didn't deserve any of this, but it seemed he wanted to be part of it. After all he had seen and heard, he was here, in her building, ready to take up the mantle of knight in scuffed sneakers.

Tonight had been a categorical disaster. She was about 90 percent certain that whatever she had just killed was the same thing she had seen with the priest the previous week. A different version of the same thing. And while she wasn't quite as certain, she was willing to stake some good money on the idea that whatever they were, they weren't human.

At least, not anymore.

She had wondered if there weren't other souls besides the ones she was searching for. Her understanding had always been that she was hunting the worst of the worst, the violent, the malevolent, but what if that wasn't wholly true.

If you're not hunting the worst, what could be worse? Liars, cheaters, traitors, none of those would cause that. *So what could have gone sideways in their possession to lead to what just happened?*

The being—and she was sticking to "being" for now—had seemed nearly impervious to pain, or oblivious to it, and hell-bent on whatever goal he had set for himself. If he had been human, something had definitely been wrong.

Of course, the same would have been true if he hadn't been human.

When Fia had invited Max back to her apartment to clean up, she had meant exactly that. Now though, enveloped in his scent, she wanted to pick up where they hadn't had the chance to leave off at the bar. She might not have made it to that restroom door tonight, but she had been down similar hallways enough times to know he had wanted her to follow him.

"I'm going to grab a shower," she announced as they walked through the door of the apartment. She took extra care to lock the door behind them, the memory of the bird still fresh in her mind. Not that a deadbolt would have stopped the bird, but since everything else had gone wrong, she didn't want to take any chances.

She took a dozen steps past Max and stopped. She waited with her back to him and counted to ten before stripping out of her clothes, leaving them to lie where they fell, and continuing down the hall.

"Oh, wow! You got the door fixed already." His voice followed her, and she smiled at the metallic thunk of his belt hitting the hardwood floor.

Sixteen

Max picked Fia up and laid her, naked, across the blankets of the enormous bed, climbing up to lie beside her. Their hair was still wet from the shower, their clothes still on the floor of the living room.

He propped himself up on one elbow and traced a finger over the muscles of her stomach. "Tell me everything you think I should know about Fia Drake."

She stared at the ceiling, half-hypnotized by the fan, enjoying the caress of his fingers over her skin. "I think you might already know more than you should."

"How's that?"

"My normal is . . ." She considered the next word for a long moment.

"Complicated?" he offered.

"Not for me. It's all I've ever known. But bringing you into it—or anyone—it's a lot to process."

"That man. What was that? You knew exactly what to do. And the phoenix. I think I've already processed a lot. I think I deserve some backstory. You said you'd tell me something if I came here with you."

"You're right. You do. I just don't know where to start."

He lay back against the bed beside her, pulling her into him. "Don't worry about it. Tell me whatever you can handle, when you can handle it. I'm guessing you've never had to explain it to anyone before."

"Everyone who knows taught me what I know. Or . . ." She let the thought fade away, hoping he wouldn't press the issue. He didn't. "You smell amazing."

"I would hope so. I used your shampoo."

"It's not that. It's just you. Your skin." She rolled over and climbed on top of him. She leaned down and pressed a deep, hungry kiss to his full lips, pulling his lower lip in between her teeth and nibbling at it firmly.

When Fia was a teen, Felix—the only boy among the orphans at the convent—had been a convenient guinea pig; the two of them had explored one another's bodies in closets and deep in the forest behind the convent. Later, Fia had joined Rylan in the back of a car that was a class project for automotive shop, not long after breaking his nose with her fist.

Beyond them, she had made a practice of never being physical with any man more than once. Once was good. They got off, she got off, and they went on with life. A second time was the creation of a habit. The formation of ties.

She didn't like ties. She didn't like the idea of bringing anyone into this life who didn't belong. She was a dragon. Fierce. Dominant. Solitary.

But everything about this man lying beneath her felt so good. His body, of course, and the way he touched hers, but also the way he treated her. Like she was human.

Picking up anonymous men in bars felt good physically, but she knew none of them had any respect for her. Which was fair; in most cases, she didn't respect them either. She knew she was just as much a predator as she was prey. She fed off them, using their heat and flesh to distance herself from the death that surrounded her, to reconnect with her own soul.

Max wanted to do that without touching her. He wanted to know her. He had enjoyed the rush of anonymous sex, but it wasn't what satisfied his lust, at the end of the day. He lusted for someone with whom he could share more than heat and heartbeats.

Fia couldn't help but feel different with him between her thighs. She felt . . . human. Normal.

She rolled her hips into his, urging him inside her, and he rubbed his hands up and down her bare back, drawing her weight down on top of him. He breathed a sigh she interpreted as both contented and aroused, and she smiled wolfishly. His hands gripped her hips, bracing them, guiding her, encouraging her. She resisted him, though, choosing instead to hover above him, holding his eyes with her own, as her body burned with something that extended beyond passion.

With his hands firmly on her hips, he let her roll into him, pressing hard against her body, moaning gently with each downstroke. But only for a few minutes. With a heavy sigh, he moved his grip to the middle of her back and drew her down with enough strength, she was forced to stop what she was doing.

"Just lie here with me," he whispered into the curve of her neck, pulling her to lie against him.

She complied, laying her head on his chest. His heart beat in her ear, and she closed her eyes to listen to it.

Human.

"I think I've figured out something else," he whispered into her hair. She turned to meet his eyes. "Sex."

"What about it?"

"You're a fan." His grin was mischievous and playful, but it faded quickly. "But just as much as you enjoy sex, I think it serves as an escape for you. Something totally fucked up just went down in your life, and your response is wanting me—or someone—to make you scream in the shower. The acoustics in there, by the way, are insane. Then things get serious in our conversation out here, and you use your hips to change the subject. Another aside: it is a very difficult distraction to resist."

She pulled away from him and sat up, taking a long moment to study his gentle face. She drew a hand over his chest and sighed. "I think you should go." She got up and crossed to the dresser, slipping into a clean pair of panties. From a box in the top drawer, she produced a ten-dollar bill, extending it toward him without looking. "Cab fare. I owe you. And take the shirt."

He joined her, standing naked behind her. Sliding one arm around her waist, he squeezed her softly and took the bill from her, laying it on top of the box it had come from. "If you really want me to go, I'll go. But for what it's worth, unburdening yourself of some of it—any of whatever it is— might be cathartic. I kind of get the impression you've carried a lot of shit for a lot of years." When she didn't answer him, he pressed a kiss to the top of her head. "Think about it, okay? I'll be back in three weeks." He let his fingers slide across her stomach and showed himself out.

She gave him time to dress, listening for the door to latch behind him, before following him out. She flipped the deadbolt and gathered up her discarded clothes, including the shirt she had offered him. She pulled her phone from the pocket of her jeans, half hoping she would have a message—from Father Anonymous, from the drop box, from the news—about what had happened downtown.

Finding nothing, she carried the whole pile back to her room. She plugged the phone into the charger, dropped the clothes into the hamper, and crawled into bed. Shards of moonlight illuminated the blades of the ceiling fan, and she focused on it, trying to fill her brain with its steady rhythm.

She let her eyes drift closed. Darkness replaced the silver streaks, and in the span of a breath, the darkness melted into chaos.

Staring back at her from the rearview mirror, green eyes shone wet with tears that spilled onto her cheeks. Over her shoulder, in the seat behind her, she could see blood pooling on the upholstery, soaking the t-shirt of the young man who had followed her to a place he never should have been.

"Stay with me," she begged the reflection in the mirror. "Don't you leave me. Don't you fucking die on me."

In the mirror, she watched the young man's torso with one eye, trying to keep the other on the road as she sped out of the forest, rocks thunking hollowly against the car's undercarriage. Through her panicked tears, she struggled to determine if his chest was still moving, if he was still breathing.

She cried out to him again.

The air in the car changed subtly, growing silent. The sound of the engine faded into the far distance, replaced by a soft hum. A brilliant, warm white light grew through the cabin of the car, disappearing as quickly as it had appeared.

She cried out to him again. "You hang on, damn you. Don't you let go on me. . . . Don't you dare let go on me. . . . Don't you let go."

Fia heaved a labored sigh and set her feet on the floor. She looked at the clock on her phone.

Four in the morning.

An hour to the bunker and an hour back would put her at the Sapphire House by six.

She dug out an overnight bag from the closet, threw on a pair of jeans, and selected one of a handful of shirts she owned that suited a person with her annual income. She had felt a little nauseated spending fifty dollars on a single t-shirt, but she had found a use for it, once or twice. She needed a room at the hotel, and she needed the staff to believe they would be foolish to turn her—or her money—away.

From the top dresser drawer, Fia produced a black credit card that she used in the same circumstances that called for her to wear the shirt. She put it in a wallet instead of her pocket, put the wallet in the overnight bag, and set off out of the apartment.

When she reached the bunker, she pulled the Scout into the space outside and headed down, her overnight bag in tow. From the steel cabinet, she stuffed the bag with three rubber weights that were shaped like pyramids and had steel eye screws in the top—anchors for the rigging she was going to pack into a tripod case. To justify the tripod case, she packed remote spy cameras and trip wire into a camera bag.

All she needed to complete the traveling artist look was the guitar case.

She loaded the gear into the SUV and started toward the blue-gray haze of predawn.

Seventeen

Fia pulled into the hotel parking lot and marched into the lobby like she owned the place. She was far less likely to get someone to let her check in at six in the morning if she was sheepish and tentative. Confidence ruled the world.

Money helped.

She slipped up to the front desk. Behind it, a woman about Fia's age, with dark skin, eyes, and hair, smiled brightly. "Checking out?"

"Actually, I was hoping to check in. I know it's irregular, but I've been through hell trying to get here. I was supposed to get in last night, but there was a guy on our plane. We had to make an emergency landing, then wait for the feds. Anyway, long story short, I just got off a plane, and I'd love nothing more than a shower and a bed."

She held the woman's eyes for another beat, giving her the chance to say no, before plowing the rest of the way through her story.

"I'll pay for last night for the early check-in. Just please tell me you have a room." Fia plunked her black card on the counter to punctuate her statement and emphasize why she wanted a room here instead of the no-tell motel.

The woman, whose name tag read Nayima, paused another second, looking from the card to Fia's face. Fia hadn't looked in a mirror, not directly, but she figured her face would sell her story. She felt like she had been through the wringer.

"I'll see what I have, Ms. . . ."

"Drake. Thank you so much."

Nayima punched a few keys on her keyboard and traced her finger over the computer screen, looking back at Fia a couple of times during the process. Fia stretched her neck and shoulders, both because they needed it and to further sell her story.

"You're in luck, Ms. Drake. I have a room available right away."

They exchanged all the necessary information, getting Fia checked into a hotel where people had died recently. Nayima finalized the interaction with an explanation of how the key card worked in the elevator.

"You'll need it to access any floor other than the lobby. Just wave the magnetic strip over the little sensor beneath the button panel, and you'll be ready to go."

"Great. Thanks."

"Would you like a porter to help with your luggage?"

"No, I can manage."

"Very well, Ms. Drake. Is there anything else I can help you with?"

Stop calling me Ms. Drake, she thought. Aloud, she confirmed she was set and made her way back to the front door to retrieve her bags from the car.

She was met at the doors by a young man dressed in the same blue and gold semiformal wear as Nayima—creased black slacks, a black shirt so crisp, Fia thought it might break if he dropped it, a blue silk vest, and a gold bow tie. "Valet," he announced, his hand outstretched.

She hadn't thought that part all the way through. "Um, yeah." She reluctantly passed over the keys, not wholly comfortable leaving someone else in charge of her vehicle.

"Room number?"

She looked at the little envelope containing her key card. "Fourteen-oh-eight." He scribbled the number on a tag, along with the words *red Intl Sct* and her license plate number, and clipped it onto her key ring.

"You can call us from your room—pound three—and we'll meet you at the door."

"Wow, great."

She felt strangely vulnerable as she watched the young man climb inside her car and drive into the garage. She slung her luggage over one shoulder—overnight first, then tripod and camera case—hefted the guitar case over the other shoulder, and proceeded back into the hotel.

Her steps stuttered as she caught a glimpse of her target crossing the lobby toward her, slipping his wallet into his breast pocket.

He was a slight man, only a little more than a hand's width taller than Fia, with deeply sunken cheeks. He looked like she felt, battered and tired, with dark blue shadows around his eyes, which she knew from his fact sheet had been his normal state before possession. Living, Marshall Wallace had been a recluse who suffered from multiple mental health diagnoses, not least of which was agoraphobia. Yet he had owned three hotels before he was thirty.

Fia wondered sometimes how the souls chose their hosts, if they continued to choose hosts similar to them until they were caught. There had been another eccentric hotelier famous for murdering his guests a century and a half earlier. Maybe this was his way of picking up where he had left off.

She took a step to the side, toward Marshall Wallace, kicking the idea from her mind as quickly as it had invaded. She let the bags slip from her shoulder, dropping the camera bag in front of him. She timed the whole motion so he'd have no choice but to bump into her.

"Watch where you're going!" he growled, straightening his coat. He glowered down at her, hazel eyes she doubted had ever been considered bright now clouded around the edges. The possession was advanced. She didn't have a lot of time. "You need to be a guest to be in here."

She flashed her key card and her best congenial smile. "Just got in from a long flight and checked in this morning."

He studied her face for another long moment, long enough that she wondered if he had seen her the day before. "Very well," he acquiesced. "Just watch where you're going. I don't have time to deal with delays."

"Hey, aren't you Marshall Wallace? You own this place, right? Good for you! You're so young. That's exciting."

"If you'll excuse me—"

"I *really* appreciate the hoops your girl over there jumped through to get me this room. Don't come down on her. I'm paying for the extra night. That was the deal breaker. Or maker? Oh, I don't want her to get in trouble. You're really kind of an icon in this biz."

He made no effort to hide his impatience with Fia's chitchat. "Fine. It's fine. Please get out of my way." He sidestepped her and made his way through the automatic doors.

"Nice guy." She moved toward the elevators, hoping he was on his way to one of the other properties and wouldn't be back for a while. She was definitely on his radar now. Of course, there was no guarantee he'd take the bait, but she couldn't think of any other way to catch him alone. Watching him put his wallet away, she had considered trying to steal it and, subsequently, his key card, which she would probably need to gain access to his private floor. Ultimately, she had decided trapping him when he came to try to kill her would be the better way to go.

Inside the elevator, she hit the button marked *14* and leaned back against the wall, waiting for the doors to open again.

Her room was less gawdy than the lobby. Instead of ornate Queen Anne chairs, there were two mid-century modern cube chairs, upholstered in blue leather. The king-size bed wore a blue duvet, printed with a brocade pattern in a darker shade of blue. Outside of that, it looked like any other hotel room. A long, low chest of drawers supported a large flat-screen television and concealed a mini refrigerator inside. In an alcove just inside the room, a little bar was set up with a single-cup coffee maker and a small selection of coffees and teas.

She popped one of the little cups into the machine and filled it with water before unburdening herself of her load. Soon, the smell of coffee filled the room, and she found herself considering a trip back downstairs to explore the complimentary breakfast.

However, she didn't know how long Marshall Wallace would be out of the building, and she had a lot of work to do. She snapped on a pair of cheap rubber gloves, dragged one of the chairs out into the hallway, and began scouting for the best places to position her cameras. Hopefully, it was too early for the housekeeping staff.

The first camera, she placed above the door across the hall from her own, standing on the tips of her toes to reach.

The cameras were small and rectangular, a little larger than a pack of gum. They had been black when she bought them, but after realizing they would be far less conspicuous if they were lighter, she had spray-painted them a creamy off-white. Currently, they matched the wallpaper in the hotel hallway almost perfectly.

She switched the first camera on and adjusted it with her phone so it focused directly on the doorknob to her room. Then, climbing back to the floor, she looked around for other places to put cameras. She thought three would be sufficient to catch anyone trying to sneak into her room.

In a small alcove between two rooms stood a potted *Cordyline*, nearly four feet tall. She popped the second camera onto its beige ceramic pot, once again adjusting it to catch her doorway. Then she dragged the chair back to her room. The third camera would go inside, on the wall facing the door, in case the other two missed their target somehow.

She set up the tripod and topped it with the crossbow, arranging it to point at the door and estimating from their run-in downstairs where it needed to be to hit Marshall Wallace in the throat. She wanted the whole thing rigged to fire from a trip wire to eliminate any margin of error. If she were on a rooftop across the street, she could miss and get another chance later. Here, trapped in this box, she would only get one chance for a clean kill. After that, it would come down to hand-to-hand combat, and she had had quite enough of that for a long time.

The remote trigger rig she had brought had everything she needed to set up a nonpermanent trip wire. She couldn't very well drive stakes into the floor or put a nail in the hotel walls. They were likely hollow behind the drywall anyway, so the chances of her target pulling an eye screw out of the wall instead of actually tripping over it were higher than she liked.

Instead, the wire would be strung through nonpermanent stakes with weighted bases—light enough not to be immovable but heavy enough it would take some effort to even scoot them across the carpet. She strung the wire through the hooks at the top of each of three stands, as well as around the crossbow's trigger.

Rolling up a sheet of paper, she loaded it into the bow as if it were a bolt to test the rigging. She ducked beneath the aim of the bow and tripped the wire. With a soft, ringing *thwang*, the paper bolt zipped through the air and bounced off the door, crumpling upon impact. Picking it up, she smoothed out the nose, replaced it, and set the rig up again, her memory flashing over countless hours of her life spent shooting through a dummy made of ballistic gel. Shoot the target, fix the hole, set up the shot, and do it again.

This time, satisfied that being hit by her little paper projectile wouldn't accidently kill her, she ran through as if she were Marshall Wallace coming into her room. The paper bolt bounced off her forehead.

Now, she waited.

This was the worst part of stakeouts for Fia. Waiting. She had brought a book with her, but after last night, she expected it to put her to sleep in a matter of minutes. She looked at her phone. The app would alert her if anyone tried to come into her room, but if she went down for breakfast after all, would she be able to get back in time to activate the collar?

Heaven forbid she left and one of the maids ignored the Do Not Disturb sign on her door. Never mind the murderer walking the halls; high-end hotels like this were crawling with thieves, employees who were paid in peanuts compared to what their employer brought in in revenue. She couldn't say she blamed them for waiting until guests were out for the day and then rifling through their belongings. And they certainly didn't need to be shot for it.

She decided to take a gamble on her target waiting at least a couple of hours before coming back to drown the newest guest of his overwrought boutique hotel. Turning up the volume on the app for the spy cameras, she curled up on top of the blankets to take a nap in her clothes.

She leaned against the barricade and let the music flood over her, enjoying the view of the long-haired, shirtless drummer—the drummer she couldn't get out of her head. At this angle, his trim form was partially concealed by the sleek matte-black bodies of the kick drum and floor tom, but what she could see was still nice. His long, muscular arms flailed around his head, bringing hammer blows down on his instruments, and his handsome angular face was covered in golden-red-brown hair.

Behind her, she heard a hissed, heavy breath, and then another, and a hand clamped down on her shoulder. She turned and found herself standing toe to toe with the man she had encountered the night before, his lower jaw dripping with blood as if he were in a scene from a bad vampire movie. He reached for her, his fingers brushing against her cheek, and she ducked his grip, colliding with another music lover.

The woman turned to face Fia and hissed the same way the man had, reaching for Fia the same way the man had. And then another man joined them. And another. Until Fia was overrun, her shoulders pinned against the steel fence, expecting the force of all of them combined to topple the whole works back into the stage.

The music stopped. She expected to hear questions, people wondering why the music had stopped, but her ears filled with a complete absence of sound. A pair of leather high-top sneakers landed on the fence beside her shoulder, and a hand descended in front of her. She let the drummer pull her up to his level, out of the zombie pit, as each of the concertgoers continued gnashing their teeth at her. She turned to face him, just in time for him to bury his own teeth in the side of her neck.

Fia sat up before she was even fully out of the dream. Her heart pounded in her ears, and sweat dripped from her forehead and neck. She took a couple of deep belly breaths, holding them for a five count before releasing them, trying to slow her pulse. When she felt a little calmer, she reached for her phone to look at the time. Nine o'clock. Two hours. So much for a quick cat nap.

Despite the nightmare, she did feel better than she had before she had lain down. But now she was hungry. She grabbed the room service menu and rolled her eyes. Fifteen dollars for bacon and toast. Was the toast buttered in gold? She tossed the book aside and considered the rigging on her bow for a long moment. There was a grocery store not far from the hotel.

Decision made, she released the trip wire, still worried about that hypothetical housekeeper with sticky fingers, and slipped out of the room, making sure the Do Not Disturb sign was securely in place on the doorknob.

Downstairs, she made a quick spin through the hotel conveniences to see what they might not have, then made a point of loudly asking the concierge where she could get some sleeping pills. Once outside the hotel, she scurried, moving as quickly as she could without breaking into a full sprint, down the two blocks to the grocery store. She grabbed whatever she thought she could snack on in the room or stash in the bunker later.

Once her handbasket was filled with a package of beef jerky, snack-size cups of peanut butter, and some presliced apples, she hurried through the self-checkout, hoping to get back to her room as quickly as possible. She grabbed a book of brain teasers—crossword puzzles, five-minute mysteries, and word searches all in one book—and tossed it across the scanner too. She was going to need something more active than just a book to keep her awake.

Back in the room, she restrung her trip wire and filled the coffee maker with water to make a new cup of coffee, dumping the one she had abandoned earlier in the sink since there was no microwave in the room. She tore the top off the beef jerky, stuffed a chunk in her mouth, and sat down at the desk with her puzzles.

The setting sun had started to throw long shadows across the floor of the room when she heard a loud click and hiss.

"What—"

She took a quick scan of the room, focusing on the heavy white smoke that filtered through a vent near the ceiling. Within seconds, the sweet smoke was already making her feel dizzy. She grabbed a hand towel out of the bathroom, soaked it in the sink, and tied it around her face. The sound of a tropical bird signaled the motion sensors on the cameras had been tripped, and she flipped open the app with one hand to see who was coming in, the other hand pressed over the top of the towel.

Just as she had hoped, Marshall Wallace stood at her door, poised to swipe his key and let himself in. She guessed he was waiting until enough of the gas had been dispensed into the space that she wouldn't be able to fight back. He adjusted an industrial-looking respirator—the kind Rylan and his friends had used when they got the chance to airbrush one of their cars—over his nose and mouth and slid his card into the slot.

She heard the *chunk-chunk* of the lock disengaging and

wondered what he would have done if she had mechanically jammed the door closed. He didn't look sturdy enough to break through the door. Would whatever he was piping in eventually suffocate her?

She slipped around the wall that separated the bathroom from the main space, out of sight of the door, and waited. In the second it took him to push the door open far enough to trip the wire, she imagined a dozen ways this could go wrong. Half of them ended with her putting him down by hand. The other half ended with him smashing her head on the bathroom tiles. Or strangling her or drowning her in the toilet. She shook the negative thoughts away as the bowstring popped and the bolt tore through the thickening air with a barely audible *swish*.

Marshall Wallace made a wet sound as the bolt pierced what should be his voice box, assuming she had aimed it right, and he fell to his knees on the carpet. In the heartbeat it took Fia to round the corner and drag him the rest of the way into the room, the stone-colored carpet was soaked in black-red blood and the body formerly known as Marshall Wallace was gurgling its last breath.

She removed the bolt and tossed it aside, snapping the containment collar into place. The green light came on, triggering the GPS locator on the other end, and she moved quickly to get out of the room.

She collapsed the bow, stuffing it and the bolt unceremoniously into the guitar case. She tossed her bag of groceries, puzzle book, and spy cam into the overnight bag, in which she had carried the weighted stakes for the remote trigger rig. Then she broke down the rig.

"Shit!" she exclaimed, remembering that her car was in the valet garage. She dialed the number the attendant had told her, making a quick visual sweep of the room as she did.

"Valet." The voice on the other end was female.

"Hi, I, uh, need my car?"

"Absolutely. Room 1408?"

"Yeah."

"We'll have it waiting at the front door for you, Ms. Drake."

"Swell."

She hung up the phone and grabbed her luggage. She grabbed the little camera off the planter box in the hallway and gave the one above the door a glance. It was going to have be a loss. Hopefully, no one would figure out it was there for a while. If she didn't check out of the room, no one would check it, at least not right away. By then—

Well, she didn't know what then. She hoped the cleanup crew would be able to get into the room. She guessed they probably had their ways of getting around things like locked doors. Surely this wasn't the first bounty that had ever been taken down in a hotel room.

She waited for the elevator door to open, her sleep-deprived nerves shot and her fingers crossed that the car would be empty.

EIGHTEEN

Fia used her weight to push open the heavy steel pocket door at the bottom of the bunker stairs, then leaned back against the frame. She could feel the earth pulling her down, the hold of gravity increasing with each passing second. A clatter caused her to jump, triggering all her nerve endings at once, and her entire body tingled with the electric shock of being jarred from a deep sleep.

She couldn't believe it had only been two days ago that she had started loitering in and around the lobby of the Sapphire House. It was hard to imagine how she had gone from that to intervening in a full-blown zombie attack— *Well, what else am I going to call it when it wasn't an ordinary posses- sion and it wasn't an ordinary person?*—to reaching a deeper level of intimacy with someone than she was comfortable with.

And while she had gone the last day and a half without sleep, that wasn't the only thing that had her falling asleep on her feet. The last thirty-six mentally draining hours had followed two weeks of watching things fall apart around her. Fia had never had so many things go wrong at one time.

Hell, she didn't think she had ever had so many things go wrong, period.

Even the things that did go right—hot shower sex with a gorgeous musician—had gone wrong.

At least this last retrieval had gone right, as far as she could tell. She had had to bait him into trying to kill her, which she hated doing. But with the overcautious nature of the host, whose memories the soul would have been able to access, she had had to catch him on his own turf. Thankfully, he had taken the bait and walked perfectly into her trap.

Maybe I should just take the win and let the rest go. Two fouled bounties out of an estimated three hundred was still a decent record, right?

She leaned down to pick up the crossbow that had fallen to the ground, turning the rest of the way into the room as she righted herself. She flinched when she spotted the intruder who sat on her bed as if he belonged there.

"Some guy left that for you—priest's collar, the whole show. I didn't know you were Catholic."

"Neither did I. What did he look like?"

Zeke shrugged. "Tall. Taller than me, lanky, all arms and legs."

When Zeke had said that the priest who left Fia her first bounty—and each one after that, as far as she knew—was taller than he was, she hadn't fully put together what that meant. After all, everyone was tall compared to her. What was a few more inches?

The priest who had made himself comfortable on the twin-size bed, however, put that thought to shame. Even as he leaned his torso back against the wall, his legs stretched far out in front of him, his white classic-style canvas sneakers reaching past the two-thirds point of the mattress. With a quick calculation, Fia guessed he stood nearly seven feet tall.

Besides the white shoes and white collar—a starkly

brighter white than the shoes could have ever been—he was dressed in black, from head to toe. If not for the way he dressed, though, Fia would never have guessed he was a priest. Hair a mousy shade of brown fell to just below his shoulders in inconsistent waves, and the beaked nose Zeke had once described was flanked by icy blue eyes and flushed pink cheeks. Somehow, his face was simultaneously youthful and drawn, making him look like a twenty-something who had gone through a hard life.

She could relate to the feeling but decided he had to be older than that.

Midforties to early fifties, maybe, though he had no lines or wrinkles to settle the debate. Years spent on Earth notwithstanding, however, she knew this was her Father Anonymous.

"How did you get in here?"

"I have a job for you." He turned to rest his boatlike feet on the concrete floor, hovering at the edge of the mattress. He looked ridiculously uncomfortable, like an adult on a child's bicycle.

"That's not how this works. You haven't hand-delivered a bounty since I started." She crossed to hang the bow on its rack above the bed, reaching past him as she did. He ducked to the side to make room for her.

When she backed up to the desk on the other side of the room, he extended a one-inch binder to her. It hung in the air between them as he waited for her to take it.

She crossed her arms over her chest. "I asked you a question. How did you get in here?"

Even as she asked, she recognized that she couldn't have been the only one with access to this place. *And you're the asshole for thinking you were.* Still, she wasn't ready to give the priest a break. He was going against protocol. They had long ago agreed to avoid direct contact. He had made that decision by sneaking into the warehouse when she was gone, leaving a crossbow on the couch, and stuffing a bounty beneath the cushions.

"Please, Ms. Drake, open the binder."

She snatched it from him while still holding his eyes, a beta challenging her alpha, daring him into a confrontation. Not that she wanted one or thought he would actually take the challenge, but she couldn't just let him intrude on her space without making him answer for it. Even if his biometrics were in the computer along with hers.

She flipped open the binder and found a familiar-looking photo. It was of the small, emaciated-looking man she had stabbed in the middle of a crowd. The photo was candid, a surveillance photo, and where there would normally have been a detailed fact sheet describing the man—height, weight, name, occupation, police reports of the faces he had chewed off—there was nothing.

Just the photo.

"What is this?" She had to let go of the impudence. This confirmed her suspicion; something wasn't kosher in the pickle jar.

She considered the chain of events.

She had seen the "drunk" man bumbling through the mall right before her tail on Alan Chambers had gone off the rails. This one in the photo had shown up conveniently where she had been tracking her most recent target.

She tried to remember the people in the bar she had met Rylan at. The night she had defended herself against Brent Newman. It had been a standard bar crowd. There had been a girl Brent was talking to while she played her own game of pool. Small, with dark-blonde hair that was long and drawn back into a high, smooth ponytail. Fia hadn't seen the girl's face, but from behind, she had seemed normal enough.

Was that the same woman I almost ran over?

Whether or not she had been, though, no frothing zombie there.

Fia took a mental spin around the rest of the room, trying to remember anyone sitting alone and acting . . . like a zombie.

Well, there goes that theory, she thought when her trip through the memory vault provided nothing in the way of a clue. She looked up from the binder and met the priest's eyes, waiting for him to answer.

"You had a run-in with that man, did you not?"

You know I did, or you wouldn't have asked.

"Yeah. I don't know if I did the right thing or not, but he was eating people's—"

"You did not," he said curtly. She snapped her jaw shut, furrowing her brow. "I apologize, Ms. Drake, but that is why I'm here. We want to track these . . . anomalies. Alive, learn from them."

"Anomalies?"

"We—I—don't believe they are merely possessed mortals. Unfortunately, we have not been able to discern what, exactly, they are, so we want them tracked, not killed."

"And what do I do if I run across another one chewing someone's face off? Let it chew? Pass it a saltshaker, offer it ketchup?"

"Should you need to neutralize the target to save a mortal life, by all means, Ms. Dra—"

"No, stop that. I know we just met, but not really. Leave the Ms. stuff for the Sunday school teacher."

He offered her a deep nod, a show of respect she hadn't seen from too many of his kind.

There had only been a few priests who came through the convent. It had been a convent, so that wasn't to be questioned. Sister Agnes had been an old-school nun, part of a traditional order before she requested a transfer to groom little kids to be bounty hunters.

But the kids—Fia, Meredith, Terra, and Felix—hadn't been pushed into Catholicism either. They had learned the Catholic explanation for what was going on in their corner of the world, a story that included God, Satan, and a demon they were never given a name for, but not much else. However, there had been an unwritten pact that after doing what they did and knowing what they knew, the traditional church setting wouldn't measure up for them.

Fia's time with Zari had made her understand how little she had learned from the nuns.

In not being raised Catholic, Fia hadn't had to deal with too many priests directly. Often, the ones who came to their convent in the mountains dealt directly with Agnes or the mother superior, a kind but gently firm woman named Lucy, or Mother Lou. Even Sister Cecilia had called her Mother Lou, though Agnes, of course, had not.

Those few priests had been of the same school of thought as Agnes: *children should be seen, not heard,* and *children will be told what they need to know, when they need to know it.* She had even overheard one priest—while discussing Fia with Agnes—utter the idiom *spare the rod, spoil the child.* He had thought Fia needed to be beaten more often.

Maybe she had, at that, but none of those previous experiences had prepared her for this nod, almost bow, from Father Anonymous.

"Fia it is, then. Please. If it is a question of the life of a human and the life of the anomaly, please save the human if you can. But if you can find a way to track the anomaly with little incident, that would be preferable."

"So what you're saying is, putting that thing down *was* the right thing to do?" She didn't let him answer. "You keep saying *anomaly*. Is that officially what we're calling them? Not *zombies*?"

He raised an eyebrow. "No, not zombies. This is a real threat, Fia, possibly a direct threat to you. You would be wise—"

"Hey, I had to call them something. *Zombie* seemed appropriate. But I can get on board with *anomaly* too." She flipped to the next page in the binder, but it was same song, second verse: a photo with no information. "How am I supposed to find these things if I don't know who they are?"

"You may not need to. Rather, it seems that they are finding you."

"Just two."

"That you know of. These photos are all of anomalies I have observed either actively following you or near enough to raise questions."

She looked up from the binder, eyes wide, brain screaming. She didn't know which part of that statement she should address first: that these zombie things were following her or that he was. As if reading her mind, he continued.

"I have taken an interest in these anomalies. I have only been following you to the extent that you have been in the same places." He paused, though whether for effect or simply to consider his next sentence, Fia didn't know. "Which is how I determined that they may be targeting you directly."

"Swell. How many have you seen following me? Actively, as you put it?"

He ignored her question, instead reaching over without standing to turn the page. He tapped the new page with a long, narrow finger. "What I can't understand is where they go."

"Huh?"

"They bump around, occasionally attack someone, and disappear as suddenly as they appeared. Which is why I want you to fit them with trackers rather than killing them."

"So this is a wildlife situation? Tag and release?"

"You could say that, yes."

She looked back at the binder. No information, just blurry candid photographs taken from a distance, the zoom lens pushed to the far end of its capabilities. She knew where they went. Or one of them, at least. Among the photos was the "drunk" man she had seen bumping around on the mall. But she didn't know where he had gone after the other priest had gathered him up.

"How am I supposed to find them? There's no information"—she turned the binder to show him the blank pages—"and it sounds like the things in *these* photos are likely gone anyway."

"Therein lies the challenge, Ms.—Fia. I don't feel comfortable leaving it to chance, letting them find you, because that could take anywhere from hours to weeks. However, because they appear suddenly, seemingly from thin air . . . well, it is going to be a challenge."

"Perfect."

Fia laid the binder open on the desk and met the priest's icy eyes. They were the palest shade of blue she had ever seen, nearly white, the color of a clear winter sky as the sun crested over the horizon to begin the day. As she held his gaze, the skin on her arms and back prickled, gooseflesh erupting across the exposed areas. At the same time, she felt warm like expensive brandy. The contradiction made her shudder involuntarily, and she stretched her neck to try to shake the feeling.

"So what *am* I supposed to do?"

NINETEEN

With the lanky priest in the navigator's seat, Fia drove her SUV to the front door of a massive cabin. It looked like a small hotel, a resort to house skiers in the winter or mountain bikers in the summer. They were high enough here in elevation, and close to a glacier, that there were still hints of snow in places where the sun only penetrated the canopy for an hour or two in the late evening or early morning.

From the front, Fia could see two stories of the cabin. What looked like a greenhouse—with walls consisting almost entirely of windows—stretched over three levels high, the first of which was recessed into the ground at the end of the cabin.

"What is this place?"

"Come inside. We have a lot to do before you can start tracking the anomalies."

"Wouldn't *zombie* be easier to say? Especially with as many times as you say it?"

He didn't answer her, only opened the SUV's passenger door. She couldn't imagine him in a regular car, not with the way he had to unpack himself even from the Scout. The thought of him folded completely in half, with his knees near his ears, made her huff out a laugh before she could stop it. He turned to her, a harshly questioning expression on his round face.

He reminded her of a cellar spider.

She followed suit, reaching for the door lock before deciding there was no use for it out here. He led her through the front door into a foyer open to both the ground and second floors. Granite tiles in varying shades of tan, brown, and cream stretched across the grand floor. Rising up from the tiles in three directions were walls and a staircase of deep red wood, and the back wall of the space displayed the same kind of glass panels that made up the greenhouse. Through the glass, she could see a dense forest of greenery, shrubs mixed with native trees, with a narrow garden path that vanished into the green.

The priest waved a hand to the right, toward the three-story windowpanes Fia had seen on the way in. "Over there is the library, not a greenhouse, though I have, on more than one occasion, questioned why there was not a greenhouse on the property. It might be good for the kids. There is a garden, however," he revised. "Sister Rebecca helps the kids tend to that . . . apologies. This way."

He turned and started down a hallway to the left, waving the same hand over his head. "There are sleeping quarters upstairs, as well as off the kitchen, behind the garage."

He didn't elaborate any further as he continued down the hall, a narrow, dark corridor with a handful of closed doors. At the end of the hall, he pushed through a swinging wooden door into an industrial-quality kitchen. In stark contrast to the deep, warm wood of the hallway and foyer, every surface of the kitchen that wasn't stainless steel gleamed in white granite tiles.

On an island in the center of the room was a gas range built to cook eight pots or six pots and an indoor grill plate. Fia thought she could have showered in the commercial refrigerator.

"Please, have a seat." The priest gestured to a collection of steel stools positioned around a chest-high steel table. "Would you like something to eat?" Fia had a vague memory of beef jerky several hours before, so she accepted his offer. "I'm afraid I am not much of a chef." He pulled what looked like a homemade deli tray from the refrigerator and a loaf of bread from the counter. "Mustard? Mayonnaise?"

"Mayo. Thank you." He placed all the pieces of a sandwich on the table and took a seat facing her. "Some assembly required," she muttered, dipping a knife into the mayonnaise jar.

There was a soft sound behind her as someone else passed through the swinging door. "Father McGregor, I was not expecting you—"

Fia felt the muscles of her shoulders tighten as the voice fell silent. There was nothing in the universe that would erase the sound of that voice from her memory. She turned slowly to face the newcomer. Standing there was a nun, nothing visible but her drawn, deeply lined face and steel-gray eyes.

"Sister Agnes?"

"Fiammetta. I was certainly not expecting you. You came here with Father McGregor?" The rough old nun's gravelly voice cast a tone of blame over the room. Fia felt guilty, despite having done nothing wrong that she knew of. It was just the effect of Sister Agnes's presence.

"I guess, if that's his name." Fia turned back to the priest, offering him a shrug.

"Many of the younger generation have taken better to calling me Father Scott. You may call me either." He set about cleaning up from her sandwich creation. "And it is Mother Agnes now," he said from within the refrigerator.

"Sure it is. Yes, Reverend Mother, Father McGregor . . . Father Scott . . ." She tried both on for size. "Father Scott brought me here. Recruiting me for some kind of wildlife tracking—"

"Father McGregor, I trust you took the proper precautions in bringing Fiammetta here?"

"Hello." Fia waved her hand between them, shifting her attention from one to the other. "Still in the room. What do you mean, 'proper precautions'? And where is here?" Father Scott and Mother Agnes remained locked, staring unblinkingly at one another in silence for the span of several heartbeats. Fia thought she could feel an electric charge in the air between them. "Um, guys?"

The door swung open again, and another nun crossed the threshold, this one small and young—perhaps Fia's age. "Reverend Mother?"

"What is it, Sister Rebecca?" Agnes answered before turning to face the younger woman. Fia studied the priest's face, looking for any sign of what had just passed between the woman who had raised her and the man who had helped her get off the streets. Finding nothing, she turned to face the second nun too.

"Hi. Rebecca, was it? I'm Fia. Sorry, I guess it's my fault Mom and Dad are fighting." She extended her hand to Rebecca, who bowed her head in response. "At least, I think they're fighting."

"I have heard a lot about you, Miss Drake."

Fia stole another glance at the elder nun. "Well, I hope maybe we can be friends in spite of that."

Rebecca nodded politely. "That would be nice."

"Okay, I guess we should get down to business, then? Or does everyone here know . . . ?" She let her eyes track from one person to the next, waiting for anyone to speak.

"Reverend Mother," Rebecca started over. "If I may?"

"Apologies, Sister. You needed something when you came in. What was it?"

"Yes. It's the teens, Mother." She lowered her voice and took a step closer to Agnes. "I—well, that is—they're— Reverend Mother, I'm afraid they are missing."

Fia barked out a laugh. "She wouldn't be talking about another batch of hunters, would she, Reverend Mother?" She spun the nun's title with exaggerated emphasis.

"Fiammetta, this is really not your concern. Sister, what do you mean, they are missing?"

"Sister Cecilia went to their rooms for bed check, and they weren't there. None of them. She is out in the gardens looking for them. She asked that I not tell you, but I thought you should—"

"Cecilia? She's here?" Fia asked, genuinely interested. Fia had liked Sister Cecilia. If Agnes had been more like Cecilia, Fia might not have run away. "By the way, where is here?"

"Fiammetta, please." Fia could only ever remember Agnes using two tones when saying her name: condescension and impatience. This was the latter. "Sister, you said Sister Cecilia is out looking for them in the garden?"

"Yes, ma'am."

"Have you looked anywhere else?"

"No, Reverend Mother. I came straight to you."

Mother Agnes turned back to Fia and Father Scott. "You two will have to excuse me." She rested a hand on Rebecca's shoulder, ushering her back toward the door. The two spoke quietly between themselves as they left the room. Fia struggled to hear what they were saying.

When they were gone, she laughed, this time more softly. "Comforting to know that nothing changes. My money is on pot, deep enough in the forest that Agnes and the others will have decided they 'couldn't have gone this far' before turning back." She cleared her throat, realizing she might be revealing more about her own youth than she should. "I mean, I wouldn't know anything about that. You brought me out here to show me something?"

Father Scott furrowed his brow, visibly considering what she had said. "Yes," he replied after a long moment. "Come with me."

He led her through a door on the other side of the kitchen from where they had come in. They followed a long L-shaped hallway into an office. He pulled a case from behind the desk and laid it open on top. It was packed with crossbow bolts, but they weren't her ordinary bolts.

She picked one up and twirled it between her fingers. It was lighter than she expected, almost flimsy. At the end was a small computer chip.

"That chip," the priest explained, "will adhere to the target on impact, while the rest of the bolt will fall away. It's light enough that it won't penetrate flesh when fired from a distance, so you can fire one of these just as you would a normal bolt, aiming for the spine at the back of the neck." He took the bolt back from her, replacing it in the case and snapping the lid closed. He picked it up from the desk and offered her the handle.

"I still don't understand how I'm supposed to find these things without any information."

"Unfortunately, I do not have an answer for that. I have merely had the luck of crossing paths with them in my daily business in the city. But I cannot get close enough to tag them with the trackers. That is where you come in."

"Am I going to be following you, and your luck, around?"

"No, I don't believe that would be wise. I am going to have to leave you to do this on your own. I can say, though, they seem to be drawn to crowds."

"So, zombies?"

He ignored the question. "They follow noise, with little to no regard to their personal safety. I have seen more than one wander through traffic, unfazed and unharmed."

"So, zombies—forget it. So you have nothing in the way of a tip, other than crowds and noise. That's only, like, the whole city."

"However, if they are targeting you directly . . ."

"Music. Bars." He nodded. "Okay, I can figure that out."

"You will be compensated."

"Damn right, I will." She paused, chewing on his statement. "How many are we talking about here?"

Father Scott moved to a bookcase, pulled it away from the wall, and spun the dial on a safe hidden behind it. From the safe, he pulled a second case, which he set on the desk in front of her, popping the latches. She ran through a quick calculation—five thousand per bundle, twelve bundles visible, two layers deep—and turned wide eyes back to him.

"Per our usual agreement, this is half down, with the other half paid upon completion of the job.

"You're estimating two dozen of these things?"

"You think it should be more?"

"I don't know. You're the one following them."

"We'll start with this."

"That's fair." She waited for further instruction. When

she got none, she made a questioning gesture. "So . . . do I go now?"

"It is late. You are welcome to stay here, if you would like. Start in the morning."

"It's not that late." Realizing she actually didn't know how late it was, she looked at her phone. "Okay, it's late. Maybe I will."

He closed the case and pushed it toward her. She picked it up, feeling unbalanced by the heft of the money in one hand and the lightweight case of bolts in the other, and followed him from the room.

He led her back through the kitchen and into the hallway they had come in through. "There is a bathroom here . . ." He swept one long arm to the right. "And you can sleep in here." He pushed open a door across the hall from the bathroom. "Help yourself to anything in the kitchen. Breakfast is at six—"

"Oh, no. I left six a.m. breakfasts behind when I busted out of that convent."

"You can meet the new hunters."

She waved a hand toward the kitchen. "Maybe. Maybe not."

"They'll be back."

"You sound pretty confident. Remember, I was one of those kids, raised by these nuns. I sympathize with their desire to run for the hills."

"They'll be back." He turned on his heels, heading back the way they had come.

"Hey," she called after him. He stopped and faced her. "Thanks."

He nodded, the same respectful near-bow as before. "You are welcome. Get some rest. You've had a long couple of days."

"How do you—yeah, I guess I have." He continued back through the kitchen door, and she passed into the bedroom.

TWENTY

Shortly after eight the next morning, Fia opened the massive commercial refrigerator, scanning its contents and ultimately deciding on something that would get her out the door the quickest. Toast with peanut butter and bananas. Remembering the culture she had been raised in, she found a plate for her toast and carried it to the table.

She had barely started to eat when the young nun from the night before passed through the swinging door. "Fiammetta, good morning. I didn't know you had stayed. Did you sleep well?"

"I did, thank you. And please, Agnes is the only person in the world who still calls me that. Fia is just fine. And you were . . . Rachel?"

"Rebecca."

"Sorry. So, you're young. How long have you been here?" Fia pushed one of the stools out from the table with her toe. "Have a seat, join me."

"I'm afraid I can't—is that all you're eating? Let me

make you something better." The young woman started digging in the freezer.

"No, that's not—Rebecca, please, you don't have to."

"It's fine. I don't mind. I can't let you leave hungry."

Fia shrugged. "If you insist, I guess."

Rebecca pulled two packages from the freezer. "Do you eat meat? Would you like bacon or sausage?"

"Um, sausage?"

Rebecca moved like a tornado, black robes swirling around her feet as she danced through the large space, setting up the grill plate across the center burners of the range. "Eggs? Fried or scrambled?"

"Scrambled," Fia said, accepting that Rebecca wasn't going to take no for an answer. She stood to join the young woman. "Can I help?"

"No, no, please. You are a guest. Sit. Finish your toast. Would you like coffee?" She gestured toward a pot that had been made earlier.

Fia shrugged and moved toward the coffeepot. "Cups?" Rebecca waved a hand at a cupboard near where Fia stood. Fia poured herself coffee, returned to the table, and continued munching on her toast as she watched Rebecca fuss over her sausage and eggs. "Honestly, Rebecca, I appreciate this. I could have made my own."

"It's no trouble, I promise."

Fia finished her toast and carried her plate to the sink. Muscle memory guided her to find what she needed to wash it. Setting it in the drainer, she turned back to Rebecca. "Are you sure I can't help?"

"Cheese for your eggs?"

"Yeah, yes, let me—" She found a package of shredded cheddar in the refrigerator and handed it to the young nun.

"So, who is Rebecca? Where are you from? Did you always want to be a nun?"

"I am from the Midwest, Indiana. I took my vows to repay a debt."

The sharp edge to Rebecca's voice made Fia cringe. "Oh, wow, sorry. I shouldn't have pressed. I just thought, you know, we could get to know each other."

Without responding, Rebecca pulled a plate from the cupboard where Fia had originally found the smaller one for her toast. She plated Fia's breakfast and, ignoring Fia's outstretched hand, carried it to the table.

"Is there anything else I can get for you?"

"No. You've done more than enough, thank you." Fia moved to the table, gesturing again to the empty stool. "I'd appreciate the company."

Rebecca quickly cleaned up from the meal, talking as she wiped the surface of the grill plate. "I apologize, Miss Drake, but I really must attend to the children."

"So you found the hunters? I told Father Scott they were probably smoking weed out in the forest."

"Yes. No, they were—no, I am responsible for a younger group of orphans. They likely will not become hunters, but perhaps they will work, later, to train another generation." Fia thought her voice sounded sad, pained. "I need to get back to them. I had only come in here to find—"

A wave of realization passed over her softly tanned skin and golden eyes. "I came to find drinks for them." She pulled a package of juice boxes from the refrigerator. "We are working outside today, and it is already quite warm. Though it is better than being in the city. Are you headed back when you finish eating?" Fia nodded. "Then I hope I will see you again soon, but I really must leave you."

"Yeah. It was nice meeting you."

Rebecca bowed to Fia and slipped from the room.

Fia finished her breakfast, cleaned up her plate and coffee cup, and made her way out of the house.

It was the perfect weekend to start her hunt. Eight blocks of downtown—four blocks by two blocks—had been barricaded off, diverting traffic around a small music festival that was sponsored by the local breweries. Two stages had been set up two blocks apart, staggering one-hour sets from local and small bands.

As Fia pulled the Scout into a nearby garage, she picked up a familiar sound. The trio of lumberjacks she had seen a couple of weeks earlier were making their special brand of music on one of the stages. Gathered in front of them was a healthy crowd, bouncing to the steady rhythm of the singular snare.

"Ugh," she groaned. "To each their own, I guess."

She found a space in the garage where she could set up above the crowd. The festival was a first-come-first-serve free-for-all. All the money came from the stalls rented to vendors, hawking everything from local produce to hand-made clothing, and from alcohol sales. It was one of the few times people could drink and stroll along the streets, with private security and city cops alike patrolling the barricades.

With the size of the crowd that had already started to gather beneath the hot noon sun, Fia had elected not to set up camp on the roof, the way she normally would. Leaning out over the low wall of the second-to-top level gave her more coverage anyway.

It also put her in the uncomfortable position of being surrounded by other cars and people. To remedy this, she backed the SUV into the space, easing it as close to the wall as she could get and still be able to lower the tailgate. Climbing inside, she could then use the back of the SUV to shield her from view.

She watched the crowd, looking for patterns in its movement. Most people were facing the stage, which was set up facing the intersection, with the crowd filling the side street. On the larger, usually busier street, the crowd moved slowly in both directions, browsing the vendor stalls.

It wasn't until the lumberjack trio was wrapping up their last song that Fia noticed any strange movement.

A dumpy-looking woman, who looked like she had put on someone else's skin that morning, was moving against the flow of foot traffic, on a collision course for the garage. As she started across the street, Fia watched her closely, waiting for her to do something out of the ordinary.

Fia quickly got her wish; the woman tripped over a man who had stopped and bent over, straightening his sock or scratching an itch. The woman made no effort to slow her pace or swerve around him, instead falling over him. She toppled face-first onto the pavement without even raising her arms to catch herself.

The man immediately righted himself. Fia couldn't hear them from her place on the fourth story, but she guessed he was apologizing and offering to help her. The woman gathered herself from the street, with some help from the man, but instead of acknowledging him, she continued on her mission.

Fia lined up her shot, realizing only as she tried to aim how quickly the woman was moving. She chose to aim ahead of her target, expecting the woman to catch up to the bolt by the time it reached street level.

Thwang. Pop.

The woman swatted a hand at her neck. No one around

seemed to have noticed, but knowing what she was looking for, Fia had seen the lightweight bolt fall to the ground at the woman's feet. She broke down her bow, stuffed it in its case and the case in the back of the SUV, and locked the doors. She would be able to catch up to the woman easier on foot.

Extrapolating which way the woman was going, Fia took the stairs from the fourth level of the garage. She swung herself down four or five risers at a time, vaulting over the railing when she had descended far enough she could do so safely. She reached the street in about two minutes, just in time to catch up with the woman in the poorly fitted skin.

She followed the woman through an alley, trying to stay back far enough to remain unnoticed, though she didn't really think that was a nagging concern. She hadn't gotten a good look at the woman's face, but judging from how hard she had fallen, Fia guessed she had left some skin behind.

Track. Don't kill.

Unless it's unavoidable.

At this point, "don't kill" was the plan. She had her knife, but it was midday on a weekend. There would be far too much foot traffic, too many people watching if she—

She pushed that thought to the back of her mind, focusing her attention on following this . . . person.

The alley continued through the next block. Fia was relieved the woman had chosen to lumber along through the alleys instead of on the street. There were people where they came out of the alley, but the risk of someone asking questions was smaller this way.

Chosen.

Fia didn't think that was the right word. She was more inclined to believe it had been dumb luck.

At the end of the next alley, with Fia still several yards

behind her, the woman plodded off the curb and into the oncoming grill of a van. In a scene straight out of a movie, Fia watched as two men hurried around from the passenger side. One was the big man she had seen with Father Creepy at the mall, when they had gathered up the other one. The second she didn't recognize, but Muscle had a discernable advantage.

Each man grabbed the woman under one of her arms, lifted her feet from the asphalt, and carried her out of sight around the van. A heartbeat later, the van turned in the street, returning the way it had come. Fia ran to the end of the alley to see where it was going, knowing she could never catch up on foot.

She emerged in time to see the van turn a corner onto another side street, obscuring the make of the van and license plate before she could see either. She stomped her foot and punched at the air.

"Shit."

Drawing out her phone, she dialed the number Father Scott had given her. When the ringing stopped, she started talking before he could. "I got one. Then someone else did."

"I beg your pardon?"

"I got one of those zombie things tagged. That actually worked pretty well. The little bolt fell apart on impact. But then I followed her a couple blocks, until a van—one of those old kidnapper specials, old, seventies or eighties, no windows—hit her head on, gathered her up, and flipped a bitch. I didn't see the license plate or the make of it. But it was definitely old. And black. Matte. What's next?"

"Meet me. I will send you the address."

She ended the call and waited for his text.

TWENTY-ONE

ia pulled the Scout into the parking lot where Father Scott had instructed her to meet him. She found him, and Rebecca, sitting in the cab of a decommissioned military vehicle Fia didn't recognize on sight.

"Park your car and get in," Father Scott instructed, leaning out the window.

"Say please," she quipped, before pulling her SUV into a parking space at the back of the lot and retrieving the guitar case from the back. She moved back across the lot and stopped next to Rebecca's window. "What's up?"

"Why are you bringing a guitar?" Rebecca asked, before shaking her head. "Never mind. Father Scott thinks he knows where the anomalies are going. While we were waiting for you, we saw a group of them pass, going the same direction you said that van went."

Fia shrugged and climbed into the back seat, swinging the case over the seat into the back. "I don't know that the van was going anywhere other than around the corner. Why do you think this group of blundering wanderers was going the same direction?"

"There is a small cave north of the city," Father Scott said. "Not really even a cave. The collar you put on the anomaly the other night lost signal in that area. Mother Agnes suggested it might have been taken beneath the surface. Sister Rebecca, could you please let the Reverend Mother know what we found and where we are going?"

The nun pulled a cell phone from a bag at her feet. While she busied herself following Father Scott's instruction, Fia continued the conversation.

"Interesting. I guess I can—I would have thought with the tech in those things, they'd be able to transmit from Hell itself."

"You're not far off," Father Scott answered. "According to Mother Agnes's research—"

"Research? You mean, no one has actually been to this place?"

"Well, no, but—"

"Terrific. You know I watched one of these zombie things rip the meat clean off a man's shoulder, right? And we're going to walk right into what might be a nest of them without any kind of recon? Plus, wouldn't this have been relevant information when we spoke about these things the other day? 'Oh, bee-tee-double-u, that collar you put on the one at the bar? We tracked it out of the city before it died.' No? Not important?"

She pressed the heels of her hands into her temples.

"Fia," Father Scott said, his voice patronizingly calm, as though he were talking to an angry toddler. "I understand your frustration, but Mother Agnes—"

"Frustration?"

"Mother Agnes has found that this cave has an unusually high sulfur output, high even for this area. A similar cave, discovered in the early part of the twentieth century, was deemed a portal to Hell."

He paused, clearly giving her a chance to retort. She didn't; "portal to Hell" was about what she was expecting, so she simply raised her eyebrows and gestured for him to continue.

"Of course, no one at the time—few at the time—believed those words to be literal, but some of the church's records suggest it might have been."

"Okay, so the zombies are . . . what? Weren't we operating on the idea they were just botched possessions? Are we changing course on that?"

"We still don't know what exactly is happening with these, as you say, zombies—though I wish you wouldn't."

"Fine. Anomalies. *Zombies* is more accurate, though, given what I've seen."

He remained silent for a moment, his face twisting as he contemplated her question. Then he sighed. "Very well. Zombies it is, then. Until we have real answers."

"Sure thing, boss." Fia gave him an exaggerated salute. After several minutes of silence, she spoke again, almost to herself. "What is the point of all this, anyway? What could possibly be gained from manufacturing zombies? It's clumsy. It should be the single best way to get caught."

The possible answers all seemed to center on creating chaos. And the only reasons she could conceive for creating chaos were entertainment—which she rejected outright—and distraction. But distraction from what?

"Chaos," Father Scott replied after a moment.

Fia cocked an eyebrow. "I was literally just thinking that. But chaos to what end?"

Father Scott sat silent for a long moment before responding. "I think the most obvious answer, Ms. Drake—whatever the intended outcome—is you. Whether this is meant to create chaos in your life or torture you for entertainment, it seems to be done with you in mind."

Fia raised an eyebrow at his use of the word *entertainment*. She wrote it off and moved on. "How far is it to this place?"

Father Scott leaned forward to peer through the windshield. "I think we're here."

The tactical vehicle lumbered off the main road onto a narrow mountain pathway that was paved in only the loosest definition of the word. They wound another mile back into the foothills until they came to a jagged outcropping.

"Cave?" Fia asked, climbing out of the truck.

Rebecca joined her, a two-handed sword clutched comically in her tiny hands. Fia let her eyes trace over the girl, head to toe, before letting out a chuckle. "Why that sword?"

Rebecca raised it to look at it. "I don't know, really. I guess it seemed a little . . . Joan of Arc."

"It looks like it'll knock you on your keister if you swing it wrong."

"Make no mistake, Miss Drake. I have trained extensively with this weapon. I do not expect you, or anyone, to pick me up off my keister."

Fia raised her hands in surrender. "Hey, you do you, Sister." She moved to the back of the Sherpa where she had stashed her crossbow, and pulled it from its case, throwing the carry strap across her torso. "So, how long do you think we gotta wait on these things?"

The priest looked at the sky, then at a cheap-looking sport watch, and then back to the sky, as if comparing the two. "If they maintain the pace they had in the city—and I don't see any reason for them to slow—I'd wager about an hour."

Fia groaned and fell with a heavy sigh against the Sherpa's front bumper. "Terrific. Anyone want to play charades while we wait?" She looked from the priest to the nun and back again. "No? Okay, then." She got up and moved to the side of the truck. "Is there a radio in this thing?"

She climbed into the driver's seat, laying her weapon on the passenger seat. Turning the key in the ignition, she dialed in to her favorite station. Soon, heavy drums and screaming guitars filled the cabin.

And the area outside, judging from the annoyed expression Fia could see on Father Scott's face through the windshield. "Whatever," she muttered and let her head fall back against the headrest. "You had *Ride of the Valkyries*; I have AC/DC."

She let the music play, changing the station when the DJ dove into some elaborate personal anecdote, and took stock of the scenery. The foothills were a different landscape from the actual mountains. This area was dry, colorless. Everything around her was a different shade of red clay and limestone. Her black-clad companions looked miserable in the sun.

She scoffed. "Could be sitting in here with me in the AC." She was thinking about inviting them when something caught the corner of her vision.

Four of those clamoring humanoid shells were ambling their way across the craggy rocks. She imagined their weird parade staggering along the side of the highway, cars taking wide swings to avoid hitting them as one drifted across the white line into the road. She half wished the whole lot of them had fallen under a semi.

"Wouldn't have helped. There's more where they came from."

She cut the engine and climbed down out of the truck, leaving the keys under the seat. She felt confident no one was going to sneak up and steal a ten-ton military vehicle while their backs were turned. She joined the other two, and together, they fell in behind the clumsy conga line.

The zombies slipped, with a startling amount of ease and grace, through a narrow opening in a craggy rock formation, and the hunters stopped short. "Should we follow?" Rebecca asked hesitantly.

"That's what we're here for, isn't it?" Fia hoped her voice didn't betray her own hesitation. "I can go in alone. I'm used to it."

"No," Father Scott answered. "We—I—brought you here; we shall stand with you. I will let this be your decision, Ms. Drake"—Fia cringed—"but I do think, if we do not follow them in, we should find a way to trap them inside."

Not knowing what *they* were and if they even could be trapped, Fia gestured for the others to move ahead. "In we go, then."

Fia had expected the inside of the cave to be cool; instead, the air was heavy and smelled of just-struck matches. Assuming the matches were the size of small Christmas trees. It was the smell of a hot springs, but so much deeper. What had Father Scott called it? A portal to Hell? Fia believed it. She ran a hand over the back of her neck, where sweat had already pooled and begun to drip down between her shoulders and into the hollow of her collarbone. She could feel it gathering in the small of her back as well, soaking through the cotton of her tank top.

The cave was deceiving. From the outside, Fia wouldn't have guessed it could be more than one hundred feet deep, nowhere near enough space for the dozens of zombie-things Father Scott was paying her for.

Once inside, she stumbled as she found herself in an almost vertical passageway. She soon decided it would be easier to sit and scoot on her butt the rest of the way into the cave. The hundred feet she had estimated from the outside was a one-hundred-foot drop in elevation. She reached for her phone to use the flashlight, but she quickly discovered she had left it in the truck.

"Damn it," she swore aloud. "I can't even see the insides of my own eyelids in here."

In response, Father Scott conjured a baton-style flashlight, seemingly from his own imagination, and illuminated a nest of at least a hundred dormant bodies. The four zombies they had followed in, unperturbed by the light, were settling in as well.

Fia turned to her companions, but before she could speak, her ears were assaulted by the whining shriek of stone against stone at the cavern's entrance. All three of them turned to retreat from the nest, but any hint of daylight marking their exit had been blocked.

Behind them, the nest of bodies began to writhe and undulate, moving in a strange sleepy unison. Blue flames licked up between the bodies. Not only did the sulfur flame not add new light to the room, it seemed to absorb the light from Father Scott's tool when he shone it in that direction.

Fia looked back up the incline to where they had come in. That route was out of commission. Even if they hadn't been trapped, she didn't think she could have climbed back up. Most of what she had slid down was loose soil; climbing back up would take some time.

She grabbed Father Scott's arm and pointed the flashlight around the edges of the cave. There was a ledge running around the perimeter that was almost too convenient. *There's something here about what not to do with gift horses.* She shone the light up toward the ceiling, looking for any other way out. The light illuminated a swirl of dust motes coming in through a small crevice.

Letting go of Father Scott's arm, Fia inched along the ledge with her back against the wall, carefully watching her feet to keep from slipping into the pit. Once she was directly below the crevice, she studied the wall, looking to see, first, if she could scale it to the opening, and second, if she would even fit through when she got to the top.

A few feet away was an alcove in the rock face. "Hey, over here. Watch your step." She beckoned them toward her and stepped past the space. "Keep your back against the wall and watch where you put your feet; there are some loose rocks. I don't need you falling into the fire."

When they reached her, she shoved them both, pushing them into the alcove. "If the fire takes off, it should blow by you in there."

"Or flash fry us." Rebecca's voice registered annoyance, rather than the fear Fia might have expected.

"Well, you could free-climb your way to the opening in the ceiling, while I hang out here with the priest."

"Just pointing out the fire might pass over this alcove or it might vacuum straight in and cook us alive. I don't have a better solution."

"Fine, then. Here. Hold this for me?" Fia shrugged out of her crossbow, handing it to Father Scott. "I'm not totally sure I'll fit through that hole. I definitely can't drag this thing through too. I'll get the rock out of the way and let you two out. Maybe I can use that tank of yours to ram the rock." She still wasn't sure how to get them back up the incline, but until the rock was out of the way, it wouldn't really matter.

Father Scott accepted her weapon and stood it on its butt against the wall of the alcove. He grabbed her wrist as she turned away, pulling her to face him. Moving his hands through the air in front of her, he made the sign of the cross.

"Yeah, sure," she said with a shrug. "Can't be too safe, I guess. Thanks, Father."

She pulled away from her companions and made a leaping grab for the first handhold she had seen from the floor, then swung for the next one. Using the natural cracks and juts in the rock, she lifted her slight frame off the floor, scaling the wall, hoping with everything she had she would be able to slide through the opening once she got there.

She pulled herself higher and higher. She could feel the scorching heat from the flames below her licking viciously at her back and legs. On her face, though, she felt a cool breeze drifting in from outside.

She reached her arms up into the crevice. If she could get her shoulders through, she would be able to get the rest of her body through too. The jagged edge of the opening scraped flesh from her back, and she swore in pain as a sticky, wet patch grew on the fabric of her shirt, but she kept pulling herself through until she was free.

Out in the sunlight—not as hot as the fire raging through the cave, but close—she didn't pause. Instead, she moved quickly back toward where they had started.

A hulking mass of a man with a black hood obscuring his face met her at the front of the cave. Father Creepy's thug. A few feet away was the black van. He must have used the van to push the rock across the entrance to trap her and the others in the cave. As far as she could tell, there was no one else inside the van.

She only had a fraction of a second to wonder what had happened to his passengers before he spotted her. Fia could see the tension grip him as he grappled with his options. She figured seeing her here was a surprise he hadn't bargained for. What she didn't know was whether killing her was imperative enough that he'd try to finish the job.

Suddenly, the ground beneath them trembled, and he took off, climbing into the van and driving away down the same road Father Scott had driven them in on. Fia took a step toward the road to follow him, then looked back at his rock.

Moving it wouldn't be impossible, but it was improbable. It wasn't as big as she had expected from the inside—only large enough to cover the opening—but it would have been impossible to move from the inside, especially on the steep incline with loose soil slipping beneath their feet.

She had just taken a step toward Father Scott's baby tank, deciding she could use it to bulldoze the rock out of the way, when the earth shook again. The acrid stench of sulfur—brimstone, hellfire—filled the air, and she and the boulder were blown away from the cave.

Certain the boulder was going to land on her and crush her, Fia tried her best to curl her flying body toward the ground, hoping to land sooner than the stone did. She fell hard into another rock, protecting her head with her arms as she landed.

A sickening pop jolted her body as her right shoulder pulled free of its socket. Her stomach heaved, and she emptied its contents onto the red clay, stomach acid and coffee tearing the wrong way through her esophagus and into her nose.

Dazed from the force of the blast, Fia took a moment to survey the area, processing the scene. Where the cave had been, there was now only a wide, shallow crater. Rocks rained down on her from above, and the realization that the entire cave had exploded slowly set in.

She tried to raise herself up, but the dislocated shoulder screamed in protest. Slowly, she found her feet another way and started back up the small hill toward the crater. Solid bedrock had been shredded by the power of the blast.

Fia walked around the perimeter of the explosion—or perhaps implosion, as the small outcropping of rock where the cave had been had folded in on itself, despite the force that had thrown on her back. Carefully, she examined the rubble, cautious not to breathe in too much of the ashen dust or sulfur fumes or trip and fall in a hole. It looked like the implosion had smothered the flames as it buried everything inside.

Is it possible for something to explode and *implode at the same time?* She picked up a rock and turned it over in her left hand before dropping it at her feet.

There was no way her companions had survived. Hell, she wasn't even 100 percent certain she had, except for the pain in her shoulder. Stumbling to the truck, she braced her wounded shoulder against its fender and, with a deep breath and a scream, relocated the shoulder joint. She sank into a squat, prepared to puke again.

When she was satisfied there was nothing left in her gut, she returned to the crater and climbed atop the low pile of rubble, kicking at a few rocks. Anger and frustration, combined with the afternoon sun, made every inch of her flesh burn. She didn't know what had been in the cave—zombies, demons, demigods—and she didn't know why, but she was certain they were at the heart of everything that had gone wrong in the past two weeks. And now, two people were buried beneath a ton of rock and debris.

She dug into the mess, tossing aside rocks and wincing at the pain in her shoulder as she did. She tried throwing a few rocks with only her left hand but quickly found that to be wildly unsuccessful. Another few tosses later, her knuckles were bleeding, the rest of her fingers were stained red from the clay, and she thought she might pass out from the pain in her arm. She conceded defeat, deciding ultimately that finding the sister and the priest in this mess was a job for professionals with heavy equipment.

If their bodies could even be found.

Never mind the hundreds of other bodies in there with them.

She soccer-kicked a rock near her foot and released an animal scream into the atmosphere as she did, holding it until her throat was raw. Then she fell to her knees, hot tears streaking over her cheeks.

She let herself remain there, breaking, for only a second, though, before she pulled herself back to her feet. She climbed backward off the mound, giving it a final regretful glance, and returned to the oversize SUV.

Twenty-Two

ia eased the small tank into a space on the uppermost enclosed level of one of the many parking garages downtown and cut the engine. She took a second to digest her surroundings, barely cognizant of the drive that had brought her back into the city. Her head was still foggy from the impact and the pain in her shoulder. It was back where it belonged, but it still ached badly enough to demand most of her attention.

She coughed, trying to clear her chest of ash and dust from the explosion. She remembered reading once about a procedure coal miners would undergo to flush their lungs out with saline. It had sounded a lot like drowning, but it might be worth it. She imagined being one of those miners, feeling like she did right now all the time.

She forced another deep, hacking cough, to no avail.

Fia climbed down from the truck and studied the keys. She considered leaving them in the seat—what did she need a beast like this for? She already had the International Scout, and she could get just about anywhere she needed to go faster on foot.

After some thought, though, she pocketed the keys and headed for the stairs. She needed to figure out what was next, and this hunk of steel might be the best bait to get Agnes to talk to her.

She pulled the now-empty guitar case from the back of the vehicle and dragged herself to the elevator, too exhausted to take the stairs. Out on the street, she headed north, pulling her hood up over her rust-colored hair. It was sixteen blocks to the apartment, but she wasn't going there. She still had so much left to do before she could drop anchor.

Her first order of business was to get the Scout, which meant taking a ride share or public transportation back to the lot where she had left it. She looked down at her dust-covered body and decided on a bus. When she reached the nearest bus stop, she looked up the route number on her phone to see if this bus would take her anywhere close to where she needed to be.

Once she had retrieved the Scout, she was on her way to the bunker. She couldn't remember ever being so happy to set dossiers and surveillance photos ablaze in the firepit outside the bunker. She was going to enjoy watching the photos of those zombie things curl into themselves and turn black as the flames devoured them.

Muscle memory guided the SUV, and before she knew what had happened, she was staring at the pale-gray concrete of the ten-by-fifteen-foot space, the stainless-steel desk, and the rack to hold her crossbows—her crossbow—

Damn. She had really liked that weapon.

She pulled the priest's keys from her pocket, taking one

more look at them. The big key with the black rubber started the Sherpa. There was also a small key she guessed would open a padlock somewhere and a couple of garden-variety house keys. She dropped them with a ringing clatter onto the steel desk and began her ritual of dismantling her surveillance.

For years, she had pinned photos and information to the corkboard above the desk, but this time, she had left everything in Father Scott's binder. She opened the cover and tore the first page from the book. Without opening the rings, she tore page after page from the book and threw them venomously into the plastic tote. Once she had gathered every trace of them, she carried the box back to the surface to burn it all in the firepit.

It wasn't until the first of the photos succumbed to the heat that she became aware of her exhaustion. And the pain in her shoulder had returned with a vengeance, exacerbated by driving and tearing apart her surveillance. She hadn't seen it in a while, but she thought there was a sling in the cabinet. She would have to find it.

Back downstairs, she tossed the tote aside with a careless clatter and fell face-first, fully clothed, onto the bed. She was asleep before she could even get comfortable.

When Fia returned to the surface, the sun was descending below the tops of the trees, and the evening mountain air was cool enough to make her shiver. She rubbed her free hand over her injured arm and climbed into the SUV, tossing the recovered sling in ahead of her. She didn't think she could drive with it on, even if driving without it hurt like hell.

She decided to let the car choose the way. Part of her

was ready to be back in her apartment, with her shower, her kitchen, and her bed, not the glorified campout she got from her brief stints—and getting briefer—in the bunker.

The romance of that had left her long ago. If it had ever been there at all.

Another part of her, though, longed for a crowd. She wondered if there was a good show somewhere in town. Injury notwithstanding, it would feel good to sweat out the horrors of the day—of the month—and thrash around in a mosh pit for a couple of hours.

Maybe even find a hookup.

Fia hadn't thought about him too much in the last few days, but now that everything had stopped moving, thoughts of Max were creeping back into her mind, and she was determined not to let them. She needed someone else, some anonymous no one, to take her mind off him before he got too cozy in her brain again.

The idea of finding someone to bring back to the apartment sealed the deal, and she turned off the interstate toward a shower. Upon making that decision, she realized just how disgusting she was: covered in dirt and ash, maybe even blood—she hadn't checked the scrape on her back. *She* wouldn't go home with her in such a condition, even after all the sweat of the mosh pit.

As soon as she got home, she undressed. Beneath her clothes, her right shoulder was deep purple from the curve of her neck to her elbow, and a similar shade spread from her right hip halfway down her thigh.

"Gorgeous," she muttered, turning the hot water on in the shower and climbing in. Everywhere the water touched that wasn't already purple turned bright red. The water pooling on the granite floor was a dingy shade of red-gray-brown, as clay mixed with ash and blood. She let the water cascade over her smooth tattooed skin, not moving to actively wash anything, just relishing the feeling of the wet heat on her nerves.

She had to force herself to get out of the shower and stop running water down the drain. She had never been thrown fifty feet into a rock before, so finding all the places that hurt was going to be an adventure for the next few days. She dried off and, leaving the towel on the bathroom floor, went to her room to get dressed. She opened her phone, idly looking for the best place to go out tonight, while she picked out clothes. She tossed a deep blue tank top and black jeans onto the bed, then sat down next to them with a bottle of lotion.

Her body delighted at the feel of the bed beneath her. She sat unmoving, the bottle between her hands, for several seconds before lying back, resolving to only close her eyes for a minute.

They stood on the roof of her building, taking in a view of the city she didn't have from her apartment. He had pulled her close to him, cradling her face in his calloused, leather-smooth hands, and his eyes burned into hers. She could feel his hot breath on her lips as he hovered at the tenuous edge of a kiss, teasing her, making her want it more because he was keeping it from her. The heat from his body was even more intense than the summer sun overhead.

He held her like that, centimeters from his own lips, until she couldn't take it anymore. He had known all along what he was doing, and she could feel the corners of his mouth curl as she bridged the distance and took what she wanted from him.

Fia woke with a start, sitting up so quickly that she almost pitched herself off the foot of the bed. The sky was a pale mixture of lavender, peach, and pink, introducing another day. She sighed.

So much for getting Max off her mind.

TWENTY-THREE

Fia reached up with her left hand to pull a glass down from the kitchen cabinet, resting the glass on the counter before using the same hand to close the door. She carried it to the sink, where she tried, at first, to hold the glass with two fingers while turning on the water with the same hand. When that didn't work, she gave up and set the glass in the basin beneath the faucet. She turned on the water, but her aim was off. The power of the spray knocked the glass over, and water splashed off the side of the glass and up into her face. She smacked the handle to shut off the spray.

With an anguished cry and a frustrated flourish, she tore at the straps securing her sling. When she was finally free of it, she pitched it out into the open space of the living room.

"Forget it! It's not worth it!"

Twenty-year-old Fia had loved everything about this apartment. She basically owned the whole top floor of the building. She had never been sure if she was more in love with the exposed bricks and duct work, the full balcony, or the giant walk-in shower.

Twenty-four-year-old Fia had spent so much of her time chasing fugitives that the last three days trapped inside had felt like an eternity. It wasn't so much a matter of not wanting to be in her apartment.

Instead, it was the quiet. And the question of what would happen next.

Everything that had come after the explosion had been done by muscle memory: driving Father Scott's Sherpa back to the city, abandoning it in a parking garage, reclaiming the Scout, cleaning up the bunker, and returning to her apartment to wash off the dust from the explosion. Even the anonymous phone call she eventually made to report the incident and suggest that at least two people may have been trapped in the area had been automatic.

The only thing that hadn't been automatic was what to do next. She didn't know how to get back to the safe house with Father Scott's mini tank and get back to the city without what was sure to be an intensely unfortunate confrontation with Mother Agnes. *"Well, good news is, I think we got all those weird things trapped under a mountain, and I brought back the priest's dude-mobile. Bad news is, he and Rebecca are under the mountain too. Can I get a lift back to the city?"* She didn't think she was ready to have that conversation. With anyone, let alone a woman who thought Fia was a menace and a failure anyway.

She didn't know if she was out of work. She had money to live on for a while, but Father Scott had been responsible for keeping her in bounties since the beginning. She figured handlers had been taken out of the game before and there was likely a protocol in place.

But Fia wasn't protocol. And she was starting to think Father Scott hadn't been either.

What about Zari?

Fia swallowed hard, pushing her guilt back. She was

going to have to suck it up and go to Zari. Surely a former hunter would have an answer for her.

She let the idea of going to see Zari fester in her racing mind for another day. Until she couldn't take the silence anymore. Until she could feel the walls of the apartment closing in on her.

Six years earlier . . .

Fia still counted her targets, and this one was number twenty-four. Her tracking techniques were impeccable, and she had followed this target to a cabin in the woods. Even having lived out here, she was still amazed by how much untouched wilderness remained outside the city.

Number Twenty-Four, a man named Anthony Pickering, pulled a girl, limp but awake, from the back of his car and carried her into the cabin. Fia's goal, if she could manage it, was to take this creature out and save his victim at the same time.

She was in the middle of tying a heavy rope around her waist when a voice broke the silence. "Fia, what are you doing out here?"

She turned to find Zeke pushing through the trees and undergrowth. Horror washed through her. How long had he been following her?

"Zeke, get the hell out of here."

"What's going on?"

"I don't have time for this right now."

She turned her attention back to the cabin. She needed to create a diversion, to get the man back out of the structure, where she could get a clean shot at him. But she couldn't do that with Zeke watching her.

She had known that Zeke knew something. He'd been there when the priest had dropped off the weapon and her first bounty. But she had tried her hardest to prevent him from ever finding out what was in those envelopes. She didn't think he would understand.

Even if he did, the fewer people who knew about this world, the better off everyone would be. She imagined there would be mass hysteria if the general populace knew there were condemned souls just floating aimlessly in the atmosphere, searching for hosts to devour.

Parasites.

"Fia, talk to me. What has that priest gotten you involved in?"

"Nothing I wasn't already involved in. Now get out of here. Get back to the camp. I promise, I'll explain it when I get back there." Except she wouldn't.

"Fia, I'm not leaving until you tell me what you're doing up here."

She didn't have time to put him off again. Her target must have left something in the car and had returned to retrieve it. This was her chance, and she wasn't going to let that girl die simply because Zeke had chosen this moment to show his concern for what was going on with her.

She leveled her crossbow at her target, knowing she only had seconds to get her shot. Zeke must have put the pieces together because he moved to stop her, leaves and branches crunching beneath his feet as he shoved her and forced a grunt from her chest. The man she had been tracking fired a shot blindly into the woods before turning to retreat into the cabin. Fia pulled the trigger on the crossbow, and the bolt flew wildly through the air, burying deep into the log side of the cabin.

Inside the cabin, a blast lit up the front windows. Outside, Zeke had crumpled to the ground at Fia's feet. She looked frantically from him back to the cabin and then back to him. She knew the girl inside was dead, likely shot in the face when the soul inhabiting the man panicked at the idea of being caught. Zeke was still breathing, but his breaths were labored and wet with blood. There was no way she would be able to carry him back into the city on foot.

"Zeke, you gotta get up. Come on, get up."

She linked her arms under his and hauled at him. He struggled to find his feet. Zeke was a full foot taller than Fia, and she doubted she could have supported his weight even if he were fully conscious. She did manage to half lead, half drag him to her target's car, determined to get him back to the city to get help.

Fia let Zeke fall into the back seat and had broken apart the steering column before she noticed that the man had left the keys in the car's ashtray. Grabbing them, she didn't even try to keep quiet as she started the engine. Her target tore out of the cabin, gun in hand and firing at the car, but she was already pulling away.

She glanced at her friend in the rearview mirror, catching sight of her own face. She hadn't even realized she was crying until she saw the tears glistening on her cheeks.

"Come on, Zeke, talk to me," she begged. "Say something. Please."

Fia snapped out of the memory. Unwilling to spend another second confined to her apartment, she slipped into a pair of sneakers and struck out into the city to walk until her head was clear.

TWENTY-FOUR

Fia lost track of how long she had been walking, but the sun had dipped below the mountains in the time since she left the apartment. There wasn't much of the city she was not familiar with, and it was easy for her to travel several miles on foot without even noticing.

She found herself slipping up and down alleys and rights-of-way between houses in a residential area. Every few blocks, a dog would bark at her through a fence as she weaved in and out of streets where she didn't belong.

It felt as if her feet were carrying her somewhere specific. As she cut between two houses, their fences towering on either side of her, and emerged into a graveled alley on the backside, she finally acknowledged that she knew where she was going.

It had been six years since she had been back here. She couldn't clearly remember the last time, but she definitely knew why she had left.

She hadn't been able to face the woman who lived behind the door looming before her. What had happened to

Zeke had been Fia's fault, and she hadn't wanted to be absolved of her guilt.

She wasn't even sure she did now. His death would never stop being her fault, regardless of how much time passed, no matter how many wretched souls she sent back to Hell. Absolution wouldn't change that. But now, her memories of Zeke had coupled with the bloodshed in the cave explosion to reinforce her belief that Max's involvement with her would get him hurt—or killed.

Fia let her fist hover in front of the heavy wooden door for several seconds before dropping it silently to her side. What if Zari didn't live here anymore? Fia had just taken a step to walk away when the door opened.

"Fiammetta? Is that you? *Ma chérie*! It has been so long, *chérie*. Come close. Let me see your beautiful face."

Fia stepped closer to the woman, warmed by her Haitian accent littered with French endearments and comforted by the softness of her face, the bright colors of her mismatched clothing, covered in patterns from all over the world. She pulled Fia into an embrace and ushered her inside.

"I apologize for stopping by so late. I was out walking . . ."

"Nonsense, *chérie*! You are always welcome. Three in the afternoon, three in the morning, I shall never turn away your beautiful face. Have you eaten?"

"It's been a few miles."

"Miles? Is there something wrong, *chérie*?"

Fia considered the question. What wasn't wrong? Innocent people were dead. She was going stir-crazy, wondering what was going to happen next. She hadn't had this much time on her hands since . . . maybe ever. The nuns had kept her busy, living on the streets had been constant vigilance, and then she had hunted souls. For seven years, she had hunted souls. Now she didn't know how to find the souls to continue hunting them.

At the same time, the last few weeks had been quite the dumpster fire. She had taken down a target in an empty office building in the middle of the day. That, she had come to terms with. It had truly been his life or hers.

But then she had had a mythical bird break through her balcony door, had stabbed a legitimate zombie in a crowded street, had nearly been strangled twice, and had led two relatively innocent humans to a horrible death, whatever pieces were left of them crushed beneath a couple ton of limestone.

Zari's golden eyes burned into Fia's. As if the woman were reading her thoughts. And maybe she was. Fia had always wondered if Zari had that ability. If not, her intuition was impeccable.

"Your heart is heavy, *chérie*. Come in, sit, eat. Talk. Unburden yourself."

Eat. In Zari's home, the kitchen truly was the beating heart.

Seven years earlier . . .

Zari looked the girls over—Poe, tall and thin, with long blonde hair tied back in a messy bun, and Fia, small and lithe, her copper hair touching her shoulders in a practical, no-nonsense bob—and then looked past them into the wide alley. "Those sirens are for you, *n'est-ce pas?* Come in, *mes amies*, come in." She stepped aside, ushering them through the door.

Inside, the smell of chilis and pork fat flooded Fia's

senses. She wiped at the corners of her mouth, hyperaware of how hungry she was.

"I will have green chili stew ready soon," Zari said, seeming to read Fia's mind. "I do hope you will stay and eat."

"Tortillas? Zari makes her own." Poe's eyes were bright with anticipation. Her change in demeanor—from controlled panic to innocent excitement—told Fia that Zari herself, not just her home, was a safe space.

For Zari, all food was comfort food. She cooked everything on her ancient woodburning stove. Everything was slow cooked or baked, giving the living space—and sometimes the crystal shop in the front—the aroma of savory herbs, fatty meats, and love.

"What's on the stove today?" Fia asked.

"Turkey stew. My friend had a turkey fatally injured and shared some of the meat with me."

Zari had forged strong connections with a dozen local farmers and rarely ever had to pay for produce, eggs, milk, or butter and occasionally got spoils from one of them butchering an animal. Even though she kept everything temporary in a genuine icebox, she did have a small chest freezer in the basement.

"Turkey. Not what I would have expected, but it sounds delicious."

From one pot, Zari spooned a heaping helping of brown rice into a stoneware bowl, and covered it with a ladleful from the second pot. She carried it to the handmade live-edge table, which had been carved from a single piece of deep-red wood. Fia pulled out the chair in front of the bowl, cringing from the strain the simple action put on her shoulder, though she recovered quickly. She sat at the edge of the seat, diving in for a few bites of her meal before saying anything.

"This is wonderful, as always."

Zari held her gaze steady on Fia's face as she ate, patiently waiting for her to speak again, to unburden herself. Fia finally acquiesced as the weight of Zari's stare pressed into her cheeks, growing heavier with each passing second.

"It's been a long time." Her voice felt weak, tired, guilty.

"Too long, to be sure."

Fia turned her eyes down to her stew. "Yeah."

With a single finger, Zari reached out and lifted Fia's chin. "Something pulled you away from me all those years ago. That something has drawn you back here today."

Fia felt a sigh forming deep in her core. The energy in this room, from Zari, was warm, welcoming, safe. She opened her mouth, not knowing what to expect from the action.

"Did you ever get anyone killed, Zari? When you were hunting? An innocent, I mean?"

A deep sadness passed over Zari's dark features. Fia watched as her old mentor let her mind drift to some time in the past.

"I think you mean outside of victims, *n'est-ce pas*? I think as hunters, every one of us who remains connected to our humanity has washed blood from our hands that should never have been shed."

Six years earlier . . .

Fia pulled the car into the back corner of a parking lot, hoping she would be clear of any surveillance out here. She raised her hood over her hair and walked around to the back passenger door, opening it carefully since Zeke's head was propped against it on the inside. She reached in as she pulled on the door, supporting his head with her hand and lifting it from the seat. Climbing in, she lowered his head to her lap and stroked his hair. His face blurred in her vision as tears flowed freely, sobs catching in her chest and burning her throat. She lifted his head again and pulled his face into her chest, her sobs filling the cabin of the car.

He had stopped breathing. She didn't need to check his pulse to know his heart had stopped too. He was dead.

She sat like that for several long minutes before wiping her face dry and pulling herself together. She knew no one could help him, but she didn't feel right just leaving him here. She looked around the parking lot. She had found a small emergent care clinic outside the city, in the northern-most suburbs. Her plan was to leave the car there, with Zeke in the back seat. She hoped it wouldn't be long before someone found him.

She wiped a sleeve firmly over the steering wheel and door handles, left the engine running with the air conditioner on high, and locked the door on her way out. She caught sight of a gas station on the next street over and cut through a patch of desert, dodging brambles and tumbleweeds to get to it.

She had never been so happy to see an ancient-looking payphone. Keeping her head low and her hood up, she ducked into the box that held it to the wall, fed it a quarter, and dialed the number she found for the clinic on her phone. When the call connected, she spoke in a growling whisper, disguising her voice as much as possible.

"Go check your parking lot. Someone left their car running."

She considered giving more details but decided the less time she spent on the phone, the better. As she hung up, she saw for the first time that her scarred hand was sticky with deep-red blood. She raised the other hand to look at it.

It looked the same, save for the scars.

She set off on foot to find somewhere to wash the blood from her hands.

Under ordinary circumstances, Fia would have thought Zari meant the figurative washing of blood from her hands, but Fia had scrubbed furiously at the blood that day. She had scrubbed and scrubbed, there in the locked family restroom of a fast food restaurant she had found nearby. She had scrubbed until she was certain her own blood would mix with Zeke's, which she didn't think would ever come off. She had scrubbed at the red blood that had dried to a sticky film over her flesh, over her scars, sinking into the texture of her scars, where she thought it would be forever.

Now, she looked down at the scarred limb, at the deeper of the crevices in the pink tissue, and for a moment, she thought she could see it glisten red with blood that had never come off.

Or with the blood of a priest and a nun, buried beneath a couple tons of limestone, shale, and clay.

Zari reached for the same hand, clutching it between her own, and met Fia's eyes. Tears burned around the edges of Fia's vision as she returned Zari's gaze. "Whose blood still stains your hands, *m'amie?*"

Fia took a deep, shuddering breath, pushing back the tears, swallowing hard on the thick lump they had left in her throat. "Did I ever tell you about Zeke?"

"He was your companion in your warehouse shelter, *mais non?*"

"He got me into the shelter. Showed me where it was, taught me how to survive there."

"It is his blood you wash from your hands."

"He knew. He met Father Scott before I ever did. He was there when Father Scott brought my first bounty, while I was here with you, with Poe, the day . . ."

Fia raised her scarred hand and injured arm carefully for a visual aid.

"Father Scott?"

"Oh, right. It's been a long couple of weeks."

"It has been six years, *chérie.*"

"Father Scott—Father McGregor—is my priest, my employer, my handler, whatever you want to say." Zari nodded, acknowledging and encouraging Fia to continue. "I met him a few days ago—for real, besides the bounties. And now he's—"

She choked on the rest of the sentence. She hadn't fully accepted the words she was about to say.

Father Scott hadn't been anyone to her for a long time except Father Anonymous, her savior, the person who had kept her alive when she lived on the streets. She hadn't known him long, but she owed him everything. Including Zeke's death.

"He's dead. Father Scott is dead—Zeke is dead— because they followed me somewhere they didn't belong."

She watched Zari's face, waiting for the shock to wear into horror, disgust. Except Zari didn't appear truly shocked by this news.

"You already knew?"

"No, no, I knew nothing of why you left. I had hoped you had found your way back to your home, back to your nuns. I had hoped your disappearance was positive, though I feared it was likely tragic."

She paused, letting the moment settle. Fia wondered if she was supposed to say something else when Zari started again.

"You say your priest is dead?"

"Yeah, we were tracking these . . . zombies. They're not really zombies. I think Father Scott thought they might be demons somehow. Anyway, we followed them to this cave, and the cave exploded—"

"*Chérie!* Do you not think you maybe should have led with being blown up?"

"No, I mean, I wasn't blown up. I got out before the explosion. I was looking for a way to get them out—"

"Them?"

"Oh, yeah. There was a nun with us too. My age, maybe a little younger. She was crushed under the rocks too."

"*Chérie*, you are carrying so much grief, so much guilt." Zari's voice was sad and shocked, as if she couldn't believe Fia hadn't simply shut down.

If she were being honest, Fia didn't know how she hadn't shut down either.

She nodded, not knowing what she was supposed to say. She hadn't really processed her current state of mind as grief, but she guessed it came in different packages. She had only started getting to know Rebecca, but she thought the young woman could have grown into a decent ally. It might have been nice to have a friend who knew what she was up against.

"What happens next?" Fia asked.

"Next, *chérie?*"

"Yeah, next. The guy who kept me working is . . . kind of out of commission."

"I cannot presume to know how it works in the network you are connected with—"

"The Catholic church?"

"So to speak. But I can tell you, the only time I ever saw a hunter lose his handler, I was in Nola. He was of another tradition as well. News of his handler's death made its way through channels, I assume, and in a few days, he had a new one. His tradition was more like yours: hands off, solitary."

"Where yours was your whole village."

"*Oui.* In Haiti, everyone was connected to the souls. If they were not actively hunting as I was, they were training hunters in some way. As schoolteachers, archery coaches. Or they just supported the rest of the village, but yes, everyone knew. It was not the secret it is among the Latin- and Christ-based religions."

"So I shouldn't have to wait more than a few more days to get another bounty?"

"I am not guaranteeing that. That is only my observation of one incident."

"I should feel guilty that I'm worried about bounties when two people are dead because they followed—"

"Stop there."

"Huh?"

"Back up to 'two people are dead,' and stop there. They did not follow you without knowing the risks to their own safety. They followed you willingly, *chérie*, because you are a warrior, a dragon. You did not force them."

The guilt in Fia's chest was not eased by Zari's words, though she knew they were right. It wasn't her fault. Not logically. But Rebecca, at least, had to have a family somewhere who would want to know what had happened to her.

They would blame Fia. They wouldn't understand that Rebecca had followed her willingly.

"You cannot think that way, *chérie*," Zari whispered. Fia's brow furrowed, the way it did any time she couldn't decide what Zari was responding to. "You are not to blame. You will break your own heart thinking that way. And mine."

Fia pushed her bowl away. "Maybe I shouldn't have come here. I'm sorry. I should go." She stood to leave the table.

"*Chérie*, I understand you are upset. Anyone would be. You have suffered an unfortunate loss. But loss should not make us lonely. Loss should encourage us to bring others closer. Embrace love that is offered to you. You do not need to face this alone."

Fia stood looking down into Zari's kind, warm face. From the first moment they met, Zari had been nothing but welcoming to Fia, taking her in despite the sound of sirens following her. She sat back down.

"Would you like to talk about something else?" Zari asked after a moment.

"I would. I just don't know what that would be."

Zari reached out and pushed Fia's bowl back to her. "Finish. When you are through, come sit with me in the soft chairs. Maybe then you will know what else you want to talk about." She got up and removed herself from the room, leaving Fia to eat alone.

When Fia was finished, she washed out the bowl, leaving it on the towel beside the sink. She crossed through to the sitting room. A pair of overstuffed red armchairs flanked a hand-carved table, all of which faced a hand-carved rocking chair. Fia knew there was a matching rocking chair in the basement, in a bedroom decorated for a pair of small children she had never met.

Fia lowered herself into the rocker as Zari returned

through the curtain that separated the apartment from the shop. Zari held her hands out to Fia. At Zari's urging, Fia did the same. Zari dropped a beaded bracelet into her waiting hands. Cloudy-clear and brown gemstones alternated around the simple creation.

"What is this?" Fia asked.

"Crystal quartz—the cloudy ones—and Apache tears. To aid in healing. Wear them on your left wrist. It'll connect them to your heart." She slipped the bracelet over Fia's hand. "I chose smaller stones for you; I thought they would suit you better."

"I can't take this—"

"Hush. I made it for you."

Fia eyed the bracelet. Even though it was incredibly simple, Zari couldn't have thrown it together in the ten minutes she had been out of the room. "You made it for me?"

"I knew in my heart, *chérie*, that grief and guilt had pulled you away from me. I had hoped you would return when your grief had either waned or grown to be more than you could bear. Of course, in the former instance, you would not have needed this, but that would have been an acceptable exchange, *oui*?"

Fia nodded. "I guess that makes enough sense."

Zari took her place in one of the armchairs, lighting the oil lamp on the table. "It has been far too long, Fia. Tell me about your life now. Assure me you are well."

TWENTY-FIVE

Fia followed Kristina Masterson into the garage across the street from her office building. With the blonde woman's crippled gait, Fia struggled to stay back far enough to remain unnoticed.

Just as Zari had suggested, it had only taken a few days—one week, to be precise—for another handler to take over where Father Scott had left off. This one did things a little differently, which Fia was going to have to get used to.

As far as she could tell, the new guy was up to speed on the drop box system and fine with using it. For now, anyway. Instead of five thousand in fifties, though, he had left her fee in larger bills, which were harder to spend on the fly. She'd have to talk to him about that.

The fact sheets she had been given for Kristina Masterson were different as well, with less information. She had thought the police reports Father Scott used to give her had been standard practice, that all handlers must have a connection inside the police department. But where Kristina Masterson was concerned, there was barely a description of the car crash that had spared her life, even as it claimed those of her sister and two small children.

The differences were subtle enough not to warrant outright complaints. But they were different, and Fia expected to undergo an adjustment period before she was used to how the new guy did things.

The transition, however, had cost time. There was no exact science to pinpointing the moment of possession, but typically, these malicious, violent entities didn't let a lot of grass grow before acting. The host bodies didn't last forever, and the period of viability was limited.

A limit the soul possessing Kristina Masterson had just run up against.

Ten yards from her car, Kristina Masterson fell to her knees and began coughing up blood onto the asphalt. Fia stopped short, startled. She took a step closer to the heaving form but started when Kristina Masterson turned to face her. Blood covered her mouth and chin, and she held a clump of hair in her hand. Her once-brown eyes were clouded over and lifeless. If her grasping hand hadn't found Fia's arm without faltering, Fia would have guessed she was completely blind.

"Hello?" Kristina Masterson's voice sounded like she had swallowed a bucket of crushed glass. "Help me. Who's there? What's happening to me? Help me."

The plaintive cries weren't coming from an ancient soul; they were coming from a living human. Or rather, a mostly living human. A mostly living human who was decaying right before Fia's eyes. A mostly living human who wanted Fia to help her. But Fia knew there was nothing she could do. The body was dead; her mind just hadn't figured it out yet.

Fia shook her arm free of the woman's grasp. She barely recognized the face staring back at her as human. Besides the clouded-over eyes, the woman's cheeks had collapsed in. Her once-full lips were white and cracked, as if all the moisture had evaporated from her body. She clawed at her head, pulling free more handfuls of hair, to which the scalp was still attached, creating a macabre extension.

"It is a sight to behold, is it not?"

The voice, a deep masculine basso with a lightly musical lilt, shattered Fia's thoughts and pulled her attention away from the body writhing at her feet. A dozen feet or more away stood an extremely tall man; Fia didn't think her head would reach much above the lower edge of his rib cage. He stood in the shadows, just out of reach of the sun peeking through the open walls of the parking structure, and his obsidian skin seemed to absorb light. He wore a black suit with a black shirt and a blue tie so dark, it was nearly black as well. The only other color visible was the glittering gold of topaz in his eyes.

"Beg your pardon?" she managed after a long moment.

He jerked his chin toward Fia's failing target. Kristina Masterson had given in to the physical death and was no longer fighting to survive, no longer begging Fia for help. Instead, she lay crumpled on the asphalt. All other sounds— the perpetual music of the city—had faded from Fia's consciousness, replaced by an electric hum and the ragged rattling of Kristina Masterson's final breaths.

Fia turned back to the man, her eyes wide beneath her furrowed brow. "Is—was she . . . ?" She didn't even know what she wanted to ask or what made her think this strange man would have any answers.

"Alive?" he offered. "Did you think she was not?" His face shifted in realization. "Ah, you did. You were taught the souls extinguish the mortal's life functions, only keeping viable what they need to carry out their vice." He rubbed a large hand over his pointed chin. "That is . . . that is less than accurate."

"Less than—how can it be 'less than accurate'? Dead is dead."

But that's not true either, her own brain interjected.

The man smiled, baring teeth that glowed white even in the heavy shadows, but offered no response. Fia glanced back at Kristina Masterson, the woman whose face had come to her out of a manila envelope in a secure drop box in the suburbs. The face that had harbored a centuries-old fugitive from the prison of the damned and given that fugitive the means to murder the family of its host.

"Mortality is so fragile." The man spoke softly, as if to himself, though with a resonance Fia thought could be heard all the way in Wyoming. "But you, Miss Drake, would know that better than most."

"Who are you?" Fia felt like she was just throwing questions into the air. "How do you know me?" Had she seen him before, he would have left an indelible mark on her memory.

"Is that truly the question you wish to ask? All the mysteries of the universe I could solve for you, and you wish to know how I know you? Perhaps your focus in this moment would best be turned toward your quest." He waved a hand toward her feet.

The corpse at her feet was now covered in what looked like enormous cockroaches, their black exoskeletons shimmering faintly blue and gold, like spilled motor oil, in the faint light. They crawled over Kristina Masterson, expanding as they did. Their bug bodies shifted and melded, crackling like a wood fire as they assumed vaguely humanoid shapes. Soon, what had been more insects than Fia could easily count on sight had become six or eight hunching goblins.

Their backs were covered in the same black chitin as their insect forms and segmented to allow for flexibility. Their front limbs were as long as the rest of their bodies, tapering into scalpel-sharp claws at the end.

The fire crackle of their shells was soon drowned out by wet slurping sounds as they ripped flesh and muscle from Kristina Masterson's bones. Bones crunched and snapped between the creatures' protruding jaws. Fia watched, numb and unflinching, as the little nightmares, by now roughly the size of any ordinary street mutt, devoured the carcass.

"Admit it," the man cut in as the ravenous beings retreated into the shadows. Fia felt like the scene had lasted a lifetime, but she was also sure it had been less than a full minute. "You always wondered what happened to the bodies you left behind."

She stammered, a dozen questions racing through her mind and none taking precedence as they all seemed equally important.

"All the bodies," he continued, "except one, at least."

Fia finally managed to spit out a coherent sentence. "What are they?"

"Well, now that question might get you somewhere. But I think it is still the wrong question. I think, in the deep recesses of your mind, you already possess the answer. You are simply unwilling to access it."

"What do you want from me?"

He laughed, a deep belly laugh that originated from deep in the earth. Fia waited for it to trigger car alarms, but it never did.

"To the point. That is more what I expected from you. Am I right in saying that you have been plagued by an extraneous adversary, above and beyond what you are used to?"

"You mean the zombies?"

"Zomb—that is a mortal concept, is it not? Undead? No, they are not undead. Though . . ." Again, he stroked at his chin, considering, searching. "They are not, veritably, alive either. Not in the way you use the word, that is."

The man was speaking in circles, spinning around himself, as if he were trying to explain something for which he didn't have the proper words. It made Fia dizzy trying to keep up.

"Apologies, Miss Drake. Fia. I do not take many opportunities to speak directly with your kind. Perhaps I should. Though I do not see the usefulness of making this a habit.

"You, on the other hand, are useful to me."

"Useful . . . ?"

"Aye. Have you accessed those places in your mind that I mentioned before? Those places where my creatures exist? You wish my identity as well; it exists in that same recess."

Fia studied his dark face, his golden eyes, and then homed in on the hum of latent electrical energy in the air. In the dust motes that surrounded him, swirling, dancing in the descending sun, she thought she could see a void, extending outward from his shoulders.

"Irzelen," Zari explained in the warm darkness of her sitting room, hours after bringing Fia and Poe in off the streets for the night. "That is but one name given to the beast of Hell—Hades, Gehenna— all accurate and wrong at the same time. It is Irzelen who was charged with governance over a region designated for the ruthlessly violent."

"You're him. The demon. Irzelen." Again he grinned, a human expression that now looked unsettling on his human face. "What could you possibly want from me? Aren't we on opposite sides of this thing?" He offered no response, simply kept his eyes trained on hers. Her neck was starting to hurt from looking up to see his face. "So that . . ." She waved her hand at what was now a ruined, bloody wad of blue fabric and acrylic fingernails. "That happens all the time?"

"The condemned leaves an imprint on its host that they . . . what you saw . . . savor. A little like your kind consuming fruit before mating."

Fia recoiled, curiously finding that statement, among all that she had seen in the last few minutes, most appalling of all. "Okay, gross. Let's not talk—"

She shook her head vigorously to clear it. As she did, she thought of the body of Brent Newman, folded between the toilet and the white brick wall of a public restroom, the little creatures ripping and tearing at his flesh.

"They are like me, though a lower level—within the hierarchy of immortals, they would be dogs, for example, to put it in mortal terms." He moved his jaw as if chewing on an idea. "Or perhaps grunts, peons, may be more accurate. The infantry soldiers of your kind.

"In the case of the young man you left bleeding out, that was a little more challenging for them. They do not, as you may imagine, enjoy the cold."

"Cold? Like in the morgue?"

"Is that what you call it? The undertaker found quite a surprise when he opened that drawer to examine your prey."

"No, not undertake—never mind. Doesn't matter. Okay, so they eat it all. Except they left her clothes and apparently her press-ons. Why?"

"Inorganic materials, child. Your kind has developed many materials that are inedible to the little ones. That is, perhaps, to your benefit as a species, though it leaves you, the hunter, at a disadvantage, I imagine. The more particles my small demons leave behind, the more evidence there is that something went awry."

"Did you follow me, or was this a trap?"

"Ah, yes, your candor is refreshing. It was some and none of both. I knew how this was going to end, so I came expecting to find you."

"So you do want something from me. Something to do with the zombies."

"Demons."

"Huh?"

"They are not undead; they are demons. Demons, more specifically, that do not belong here. They have no place here in the mortal realm. They belong to me. Someone, a mortal, has usurped them. I want them back. Unfortunately, divine law carries severe consequences if I take them back myself."

"Divine law? Isn't that for gods and angels, the white hats?"

The energy in the air changed subtly. The hum of electricity intensified, making the fine hairs on Fia's arms stand at attention, and she thought the temperature rose ten degrees. Her ears rang with the sounds of flesh ripping and bones shattering.

Soon, where the man had stood, the demon crouched before her. He was a larger version of the little carrion creatures from before, but more sophisticated. From his shoulders, broad enough on their own to obscure a small car, stretched fibrous wings that glittered blue and gold. They reminded her of the wings of a fly, if the fly were enlarged across a movie screen. Even in his squatted position, his black head, now covered in exoskeletal armor, nearly brushed the ceiling.

"Your affront," he said, his voice booming inside her skull, ricocheting off the bones until she thought the top of her head might pop off, *"is forgiven only because you were indoctrinated and did not know to ask the questions that would lessen your ignorance. My kind was created first. We were not cast out; we chose to*

leave. The angels—the Fallen, as your kind calls them—invaded our colony, took it for their own, and enslaved us. I am not the villain. I am not, as you imply, the 'black hat.'"

Fia held the sides of her head, pressing her palms into her ears as she waited for the vibration to stop. When she had regained control of her own thoughts, she lifted her hands in surrender.

"Whoa, I'm sorry. I didn't mean—let's start over. What is the divine law that keeps you from taking back your demons? And those things are demons?"

"A mortal has taken control of my demon soldiers and placed them in unnatural circumstances. I cannot reclaim them without being stripped of my immortality. I request your aid, as they were seized to target you. I believe returning them to me is of equal benefit to us both."

"But what about the cave? Didn't they—I mean, weren't they in the cave when it—"

"The mortal has lost control. What they have stolen from me extends beyond just what you have seen. However, I think they believe they are in control."

"Are you at least going to tell me who I'm looking for?"

"I do not know, cannot see. In the process of taking my demons, a part of the mortal has been corrupted. There is a shadow living in their soul that blocks the divine—like me, like your angel—from identifying them. Just as the divine cannot access one another's thoughts, we cannot access those of a mortal hosting a demon shadow."

"What do you mean, 'angel'?" Fia asked, then winced. "Ugh. This is all enough to make my head hurt." Rubbing at her temples, she added, "So, how do I find them?"

"You are an expert tracker. I'm certain you will figure something out."

With that, the sounds of his body shifting once again assaulted her eardrums, until the enormous creature had been replaced with a much smaller bird, its blue and gold feathers glinting in the scant sunlight. Blue flame surrounded the bird as it beat its wings, urging its body, now the size of a turkey, to rise up from the ground. With a predatory shriek, as if to punctuate their visit, the bird—the phoenix—flew from the garage and out into the clear blue sky.

Leaving Fia alone with a pile of polyester and acrylic.

Fia crushed the acrylic nail extensions beneath her shoe and gathered the clothes left behind by Kristina Masterson, stuffing them into her bag with the collar she hadn't had the chance to use. Then she started down the stairs, taking them one at a time, slowly, as she tried to process everything the demon had told her.

By the time she stepped out of the garage and back into a world that knew nothing of demons on Earth or condemned souls possessing human hosts, she had decided to let her feet take control. It was the most advanced decision she could make right now, to just walk. The demon had given her too much to think about.

The biggest being that the bodies she had been stalking for seven years—a third of her life—were alive. They were destroyed, and she put an expedient end to their suffering, but the original consciousness still existed, simply suppressed by a malevolent spirit.

Maybe it was better that way. Fia had felt like she was spinning her wheels for too long. Trap a soul and return it to Hell, only to have it walk out the back door when no one was looking. But to know she might at least be ending a dying human's suffering in the process made it seem a little less futile.

As she walked, she took note of the buildings around her. She had grown so accustomed to the scenery of the city that she didn't think she had really considered what surrounded her in years. Each of the windows glinting above her head guarded a life behind it. Bedroom windows, office windows—they all kept someone from falling to their death on the concrete below. Not a single person behind any of those windows knew what Fia did to keep them safe. Or what she had to keep them safe from.

When Fia finally stopped walking and looked around, she found that she had made it back to the open-air mall. The crowd was thick, as was usual for a weekday afternoon. The old Gothic-style clock tower read twenty past three.

Fia moved away from the clock, passing shops and restaurants until she reached a plaza. Most of the mall was contained on the street level, with offices above. A couple of larger retail chains had second floors because space was limited, but this plaza was three stories—four counting the second level of the movie theater.

The first thing Fia came to as she entered the plaza was a bulk candy store. They had the door open, and a faint scent of sugar-laced artificial fruit wafted out into the street, luring her in. A sea of assorted gummy bears and jelly beans stretched out before her, each flavor segregated into its own bin. She grabbed a bag and dug in, grabbing scoops full of flavors that couldn't be found in the average bag of bears.

When her sugar hunt was complete, she stuffed the plastic zipper sack filled with cantaloupe-, champagne-, mango-, and margarita-flavored bears—three shades of orange and a radioactive green—into her shoulder bag and headed back out into the plaza, turning back and forth as she decided what to do next.

Ultimately, she didn't want to think about the last few days. Maybe a movie would take her mind off everything for a little while. Midafternoon on a weekday, she should be able to veg without anyone bothering her.

As she studied the marquee, she eighty-sixed a few

options right off—a romantic comedy with one of Holly-wood's interchangeable leading blondes and a historical drama that would probably put her to sleep. She was contemplating the others when something caught her attention out of the corner of her eye. Hanging on the wall of a nearby shop was a heavy-metal t-shirt. On the front of the industry-standard black garment was the image of a snake, spray-painted beneath the band's name.

The last night she had seen Max, he'd watched her take out a zombie in the middle of a crowded street. He had done his part, sacrificing his t-shirt to bandage a stranger's shoulder. Outwardly, he had been calm, as if nothing were wrong, but a faint hint of panic had radiated off him. She had almost appreciated that. He had begun to seem super-human with his nonchalant acceptance of her world. The fact he had been even a little upset, despite his efforts to conceal it, had made her feel a little better.

Though she had been paying more attention to his form beneath the shirt than what was actually on it, she was certain this was the same shirt. It wasn't extraordinary; she had to have seen a hundred like it. But as they had approached her apartment with the tension in the air palpable, he'd tried to lighten the mood by sharing that it had been one of his favorites.

It probably held some sentimental value that you could never replace.

Fia turned her back on the movie marquee and slipped through the shop door, plunging into the cool darkness of the alternative geek haven. Everything a person could possibly obsess over—music, movies, video games, cartoons—was represented in some way among the racks and shelves that covered nearly every square inch of the small retail space. To say it was tight and crowded was an understatement. She had sought out stores like this as a runaway, relegated to shoplifting to get what she wanted.

She had never thanked Father Scott for helping her break that habit.

On the wall opposite the door, she found the shirt she was looking for on the shelf below the display. She pulled out one marked *Medium* and held it up to herself, before spotting an employee who was closer to Max's size.

"Hey, what size would you wear in this?"

"Uh . . ." He seemed flustered by the question, looking around as though for someone else to help.

A girl with half the buttons in the store stuck to her name tag stepped up to the plate. "Sorry, Alex is still learning the ropes. It's cool, dude. You can answer the question. It's probably for her brother or boyfriend. She's not buying it for you, if that's what you're worried about." She slapped Alex on the back and strolled away.

"Yeah." He nodded, pointing at the shirt in her hand. "Medium is good. Large, if he likes 'em roomy."

Fia studied the shirt in her hand for a second before also grabbing one in the larger size. "Can I return the one that doesn't fit?"

"Yeah, um, I think so. Kristi, can she return it if it doesn't fit?"

"Got thirty days."

"You've got thirty days."

Fia flashed Alex a smile, further unnerving him, and carried her selections to the counter.

TWENTY-SIX

Back out in the hot sun, Fia looked around, deciding where to go next. Feeling a strange pull, she headed up Broadway toward the old Gothic cathedral.

As she approached the church, the pull grew stronger, and she thought again about what the demon had said.

A mortal has taken control of my demon soldiers . . . they were seized to target you.

Who better to ask who might be threatening her than an egomaniacal priest who had been stalking her around the city? He had not been especially helpful in their last conversation, but she had gone in unprepared. Now she had a reason to be here and a direct question to ask him.

Did he know who might be targeting her with an army of demons?

Fia hesitated for no longer than a second before jogging across the quiet street against the light and across the small parking lot to the same heavy wooden door she had entered last time. The main doors to the cathedral stood twenty feet high at their arched center and were covered in ornate carvings with heavy brass handles. This side door was no less ornate, but only slightly larger than a standard door.

Inside, Fia found herself temporarily blinded. She blinked several times to force her eyes to adjust. *One of these days, you'll remember to close your eyes* before *you come into a place like this.*

A chill brushed over Fia's skin, brought on not only by the cool indoor air on her sunbaked skin but also by a rough and uninvited voice.

"Ms. Drake. I have been expecting you."

She turned, narrowed her eyes, her brows drawing together, and studied Father Creepy.

"Expecting me." It was half question, half statement.

"Ah, yes, of course. Following the unfortunate accident with your priest."

"Accident?" Of course he knew. His thug, the man in the sweatshirt who had likely left his neck on some Nebraskan football field, had caused it.

"In the cave explosion. A tragic loss, really. I never met Father McGregor, but I have heard stories of his contributions."

The priest took a step toward her, narrowing the space between them. The advance was a challenge. Would she accept it and hold her ground or step away and leave him with the advantage?

She shifted her weight, staying where she was but putting herself into a defensive stance.

"You are so untrusting, Miss Drake. What makes you think I harbor any ill will toward you?"

"Learned behavior," she replied. She wasn't interested in playing the same games they had played before. Today, she was on a mission that didn't include bluffing. "I haven't been given a lot of reason to trust people who follow me around the city. Or who send hired muscle to trap me in a powder keg."

He took an imposing step toward her. "I believe you are mistaken, Miss Drake. I assure you, you have nothing to fear from me."

"From you?"

"Nothing to fear."

A door snapped shut at one end of the hall, and Father Creepy stepped back, pulling himself into what Fia could only call priest posture: his hands clasped in front of him, his shoulders pulled back, his chin high.

"I am afraid I can't help you, Miss Drake."

Then Muscle approached from the direction of the sound.

"You."

"Miss Drake?"

Fia rolled her eyes at the clergyman and turned to his grunt. "You tried to trap me in that cave. I didn't see your face, but I'd put a paycheck on a wager it was you. There can't possibly be two men your size following those things around."

The larger man stood silent, his bulging round eyes darting from Fia to the priest and back. He probably hoped his employer would come to his rescue.

"Miss Drake, are you suggesting the explosion in the cave was not an accident?" Father Creepy reached out a hand and touched her bruised shoulder, making her wince and pull away.

"Cut the act. I know what was in that cave. I saw *you* with one of those things, Father . . ." When the priest didn't supply a name, Fia continued. "Something around here stinks, and it's not the big guy's sweatshirt. I mean, it *is* the big guy's sweatshirt, but more than just that."

The priest stood still, unperturbed by her accusations, and waited for her to finish. "Miss Drake, it is clear something terrible happened to you. If you need me to consult the authorities on your behalf—"

"And tell them what?"

"Well, that is the question. What should I tell them?"

Fia took a step back, away from the pair of men, her brow furrowing. Was it an act? Even if it wasn't, if he was genuinely concerned about her well-being, then why? Besides being a priest, because that didn't measure up.

He closed the gap again, matching her step and adding one of his own, until he was close enough that she could feel the heat from his body and hear him breathe. "What should I tell them?" He pronounced each word as if it were its own sentence, and Fia felt the hair on her arms prickle. He wanted her to back away another step, and another, until he had her pinned to the wall, so she responded by shifting her weight forward and leaning into him instead.

"Yes, what should you tell them? That you've been following me, stalking me around the city? That you blew up a sulfur cave north of the city and killed another priest and a young nun?"

"I had nothing to do with that explosion. As I understand it, Father McGregor led that young sister into the cave, and the explosion was just one of those accidents. It hasn't happened in years, but it's not unheard of."

Fia looked around Father Creepy and saw the human mountain still behind him, arms as big as her head crossed over his wine-barrel chest. His jaw was clenched, and he was obviously ready for a fight. She was, too, just not with him. She drew back, stepping away from the priest again. He didn't press this time but let her make her small retreat.

"No, I guess caves explode like that sometimes." Fia

took another step back. "Especially when someone wedges a boulder in front of the only real opening and tosses in a lighted match." She directed the last statement at the large man, half hoping to get a reaction from him, of any kind.

It was the priest who responded, though.

In a single swift motion, he had her back pressed into his chest, one arm around her throat and the other against the back of her head. The hold was designed to make her pass out, but he was only holding her there. He wasn't applying any real pressure, just pressing tightly enough to show her what he was capable of.

Her fingers danced over the hilt of her knife, but she ultimately decided to save that surprise for later. Her intuition told her he didn't intend to harm her, at least not here, not like this. From this position, it would only take a few pounds of pressure for him to break her neck, so instead, she stayed calm and let him think he was intimidating her. She considered maybe she shouldn't have pushed quite so hard. She would have liked to have kept him talking awhile longer, to find out how and where he was involved in this whole program.

After all, he knew Father Scott and about her. And if her suspicions were right—and she couldn't imagine a scenario where they weren't—he knew about the possessions. If anyone could tell her what had happened in that cave, it was going to be him.

More than anything, though, she wanted to know what his involvement was in summoning those demons to follow her. And what the point of that had been.

Somewhere else in the church, a door clicked open, and footsteps echoed through the cavernous hallways. Father Creepy spun her away from him, his face dark with rage. He did mean to hurt her, just not today.

As the uninvited fourth guest passed through the hallway, skating past them without looking up from what she was reading, the priest spoke softly, congenially. "I am afraid I can't help you, Miss Drake."

Once the woman was gone, though, he pulled Fia in again, this time with his hand gripping her jaw so tightly, she thought he might break it. "You will not survive this life, Fiammetta." He punctuated the statement with a shove hard enough to make her lose her balance and stumble back into the door with an echoing thud.

"You're probably right," she quipped. "Most of us won't." Before he could respond, she turned and let herself back out into the hot sun.

Twenty-Seven

Before he left on tour, Max had set an alarm on Fia's phone for the day his band was scheduled to return. She had given him the brush-off, sending him out before she could possibly think to ask him to stay. He had had to stop in the living room to redress himself. She guessed that was when he broke into her phone, which she had set to remain unlocked in her own home, leaving the appointment in her calendar.

Now, she sat on the edge of her bed, staring at the alert on her phone for several long moments, seeing it for the first time.

Max Hawkins has spent three weeks thinking of you in filthy truck stop restrooms and would be eternally grateful if you would touch him instead.

She wanted to be mad about the invasion, but instead she rolled her eyes, laughing at his lack of shame. Then she shimmied into her favorite worn-out jeans and black sneakers, tucking the purple laces into the sides. She took inventory in the mirror and sighed.

The bruise on her shoulder had started to fade, but where the purple-black had been was now muddled with yellow-green. She traded out her tank top for a t-shirt, a pair of rabbits surrounded by an ouroboros decorating the front.

She didn't know where she was going when she left the apartment; he had asked her to look him up, but not where. She hadn't known, until the notification showed up, if she even wanted to. She decided to just try one of the venues they frequented, see if someone there could tell her anything.

She set her sights on the first place they'd met.

Coming out of her apartment, she took a long look at the garage door before deciding to walk instead. She took the stairs to the street level, two at a time, and shoved her way through the front door in a bursting sweep.

There, she found Max, pacing the sidewalk.

"What are you—um, hi."

He turned to her, eyes wide. She had clearly startled him. "Oh, hi. Um, I was just—I just got here."

"Did you really?"

"No." He looked around as if trying to find somewhere to hide. "I've been here, um . . . about twenty minutes. Trying to decide if you'd buzz me in."

"That's a great question."

"You were leaving? I'll let you—"

"No, I was just going for a walk. Would you like . . ." She stepped close to him and lifted a hand to trace her fingers over dark, stiff hairs along his jaw and over his lip. "This is . . ."

He touched a hand to the other side. "Tour beard. At least, that's where I would keep a tour beard if I could grow a beard. I guess, tour scruff? You like it?"

"Not sure. It's definitely a different look." She took another step closer, close enough to feel his heat.

"You weren't really going for a walk, were you?"

She focused her attention on his lips as he spoke. She heard the echo of Zari's voice in the back of her mind. *Loss should encourage us to bring others closer. Embrace love that is offered to you. You do not need to face this alone.*

"Do you want to come upstairs? Did you drive here?"

He waved to his car on the street.

"Bring it inside and meet me upstairs."

She turned and, punching in her code, passed back through the front door and up the stairs. She pushed the apartment door open, then stepped across the hallway to wait for him in the doorway to the private garage. She unfastened her jeans and pulled her shirt off over her head before she heard his engine crest the ramp to the third level.

Feeling overeager, she redressed a second later.

He cut the engine, and her blood quickened in her veins. She watched him cross the space between his parked car and where she stood. Her eyes traced from his handsome face to the muscles of stone she knew his slim-fit black jeans and white t-shirt hid.

She opened her mouth; she didn't know what she had planned to say, so she was grateful when he didn't let her. He pressed his mouth to hers, and his tongue to hers, and lifted her by her hips. She wrapped her legs around his waist and let him carry her into the apartment. He pushed the door closed with his foot and pressed her back against it, kissing her hard.

She was at his mercy, pinned to the door, her legs around his back, and he held her there for several long, deep kisses—to her mouth, her throat, her collarbone. Finally, he lowered her to her feet, unfastened her jeans, and pushed them to her ankles, letting his own fall the same way.

Kicking out of her shoes and leaving her jeans by the

front door, Fia pushed him back, stepping around him and making her way toward the bedroom. He followed half a step behind, pulling her shirt over her head, kissing the back of her neck.

She stopped short, letting him bump into her so she could feel his naked anticipation against the small of her back. She considered turning to face him and opening herself to him in the middle of the living room floor. She let him pant into her hair, feeling his hot breath against her bare flesh, before she started walking again.

This time, he waited for her to get a few steps ahead. She hoped he was enjoying the view as she continued down the hallway without him.

Light from the late-evening sun cast shadows across the bedroom from the open window. Leaving his shirt on the floor, Max joined her on the bed, pushed between her knees, and laid kisses across her neck and torso, down her stomach to her thighs. She felt the three weeks of scruff rough against the tender skin inside her legs, and she shuddered into him. She wound her fingers into handfuls of hair, urging him to continue. Aggressive kisses that she remembered as soft were now surrounded by the finest bristles of a wire brush, and she half tried to squirm away, even as she pulled at him ravenously. He laced trim tattooed arms beneath her hips and lifted them from the bed to kiss her even deeper.

Fia fought against herself. Part of her wanted to leave him alone, to let him work, to finish what he had started. Still another ultimately stronger part wanted to pull him up to her. She clawed at his shoulders, drawing him up, a kiss at a time, until he pressed his body into hers. He pushed between her thighs, his eyes flashing like a starved animal as he hovered above her chest, staring deep into her eyes, challenging her, daring her.

She hooked her ankles behind his back and pulled him in, enjoying his flesh against her own and savoring his heat. She tangled her fingers in his hair, but he soon pulled them free, stretching her hands above her head and holding her wrists in place, rendering her helpless.

He pushed deep into her and kissed her mouth, pressing his chest firmly against hers. The only movement between them was in the rolling of his hips and in the caress of his tongue against her lips. He pressed his pelvis against hers, pushing her knees back with his free hand to make her feel even more of him, pushing, pushing until her breaths came in screaming gasps. He covered her mouth with his own, refusing to let up on her until her body relaxed back into the mattress. Then he let go of her wrists and rolled to the side, pulling her with him and wrapping her tightly in his arms. Only then did he speak for the first time since they had entered the apartment.

"I've missed you."

She smiled into the dark and responded with a soft laugh. "Yeah, I guess I missed you too." She kissed him, firmly, tenderly, and turned her back to him, keeping his arms tightly wrapped around her chest.

Fia didn't know how long she had lain awake against Max, listening to him breathe, but she finally decided she couldn't sleep and gently wriggled free of his grip, which had loosened considerably as he'd fallen asleep. She made her way through the apartment to the front door to check the locks they had ignored in the heat of their reunion.

An automatic glimpse through the peephole as she twisted the locks made her breath catch in her throat. Unlocking the door, she pulled it open and stepped into the hallway.

Two weeks before, Fia had narrowly escaped dying after leading a priest and young nun into a nest of displaced demons that had been summoned to target her for reasons she was determined to discover. Knowing it was too large for her to carry through the crevice she had used to escape, Fia had left her crossbow behind as well, thinking she would retrieve it when she rescued the others.

Nothing had been left of the cave but smoke and debris.

Yet now, two weeks later, propped against the wall opposite her door was a crossbow. Her crossbow. And looped over its nose was the white collar of a priest.

WHISKEY AND INK

Fia Drake, Soul Hunter Series
Book 2

Coming Spring 2021

Acknowledgments

I would like to express my gratitude to my Patreon community, whose support helps to make this series possible:

Founding Legacies
Patricia Harris
Redbird Stormcrow

Concrete and Chords
Glenda Pearl Kilgore

Mortar and Monitors
Caroline Barnette

Thank you to Grant Champion, Michael Guzman, Tracey Love, and Melissa Tapp for beta reading an early version of this book before I decided to publish traditionally.

Thank you to my Facebook readers community, D. Gabrielle Jensen's Rockstar Readers, for answering endless hypothetical questions and helping me choose titles and covers, even though I didn't use them in the end.

Thank you to everyone at Balance of Seven for this opportunity and especially to Ynes Freeman for pushing me to consider traditional publication.

Thank you to Robin Stevens for all—*all*—your support: moral, financial, and otherwise.

About the Author

What began with a princess captured by a pirate and rescued by a dragon has developed into D. Gabrielle Jensen's lifelong fascination with stories of the unexpected and unexplored. She has dabbled across many styles and genres, but whether through startling, staccato works of pulp horror or the dirt and grime of urban fantasy, she always finds her way back to speculative fiction.

An award-winning bestseller, D. is built from drumbeats and hot asphalt. Even as an imaginative child in the rural mountains of Colorado, she felt pulled to the chaos and clamor of The City—any city, every city. With this in mind, she aims to infuse her work with mortar and music. Her favorite views of any city are from the rooftops and the side streets. She strives to show the beauty of both in her stories, urging you to walk the streets with her as she introduces you not only to powerful heroines and antiheroines but to the buskers, bartenders, and baristas who make up the fabric of every city.

If writing be her first love, music is the trusted friend D. turns to when that love forgets her birthday. She can sing along with new songs before they've finished playing and set up a drum kit blindfolded. She can't remember a time when she didn't know how to play her parents' vinyl records. She has one Spotify playlist (out of many) that can run for two full days without repeat and an active hatred for paperless concert tickets. She works that love of music into her writing through allusions to lyrics in imagery, characters named after songs and musicians, and behind-the-scenes playlists. She will even write to a metronome if she needs to give a scene just the right cadence.

D. loves things that begin with the letter *C*—coffee, cats, cities, conversation, concerts—and things that don't—airports, humans, macrophotography, urban decay, macro-photography of urban decay, and the beauty of flaw. She encourages everyone to join her across social media and on Patreon. Strike up a conversation. What are you waiting for?

www.patreon.com/writerdgabrielle

www.instagram.com/writerdgabrielle

www.facebook.com/writerdgabrielle

www.twitter.com/writerdgabriele

9 781947 012073